On the Edge of the Desert

ILLINOIS SHORT FICTION

On the Edge of the Desert

Stories by Gladys Swan

UNIVERSITY OF ILLINOIS PRESS

Urbana   Chicago   London

© 1979 by Gladys Swan
Manufactured in the United States of America

"Losing Game," read at the Seventh Annual Conference on Twentieth Century Literature, Louisville, Ky., February, 1979

"Ghosts," *Colorado Quarterly,* vol. 20, no. 3, Winter, 1972

"Rest Stop," *Cumberlands,* vol. 15, no. 1, Spring, 1978

"The Peach Tree," *Maine Review,* vol. 3, no. 1, January, 1977

"In the True Light of Morning," *Great Lakes Review,* vol. 4, no. 1, Summer, 1977

"Flight," *Virginia Quarterly Review,* vol. 48, no. 3, Summer, 1972

"On the Edge of the Desert," *Dragonflies,* Fall, 1979

Library of Congress Cataloging in Publication Data

Swan, Gladys, 1934-
  On the edge of the desert.

  (Illinois short fiction)
  CONTENTS: Losing game.—Decline and fall.—Ghosts.—Unraveling.
—Rest stop.—The wayward path. [etc.]
  I. Title.
PZ4. S969950n [PS3569.W247] 813'.5'4 79-15858
ISBN 0-252-00780-3
ISBN 0-252-00781-6 pbk.

For Andrea and Leah

Contents

Losing Game

Turn the things out of a man's pockets and take their testimony: a soft brown leather billfold worn to limpness without ever having been made fat with prosperity, home of a few snapshots, social security card, driver's license, expired; a gadget combining pocket-knife, corkscrew, and can opener; a book of matches; a pocket comb with teeth broken out; the stub of a pencil; an old pocket watch with the staff gone, around the house for years lying broken—his father's and now his, therefore a piece of inheritance; a letter, the last his father had written, the address more than five years old; two quarters, three dimes, and four pennies. His belongings—down to the lint in his pockets. Uneasy from the lightness of his jacket, he stood, missing something, as though he weren't all there. They dumped the stuff on the desk and let it sit in a little heap while they dug out a few facts—to hold against him, he supposed—to clinch the evidence of what they'd found on him.

Name? Jason Hummer. He'd have lied if his things hadn't been such a dead giveaway, his principle being never to tell the truth if it gave somebody a hold over you. But he wasn't sure the lie would make that much difference. Another name, another man? Jake Hemphill, suppose. He saw a school janitor sweeping slow, eyes wedded to wastepaper and wads of chewing gum. John Harding: solid sort—bust a man in the crockery for making eyes at his wife; good provider. Junius Holloway: banker, pillar of the church, a power in the town; storm cloud by day, pillar of smoke by night. Jay

Hay: playboy—white convertible, leopard-skin seat covers; a creature of speed and spring and back-seat quick-hand. Nope, for better or worse, he was stuck with himself.

Age? Twenty-eight. Hair, brown; eyes, brown. Distinguishing marks and characteristics? None. No visible scars, birthmarks, carbuncles, tics, tattoos, hardly even a mole of any size or interest. True, he was looking a bit shaggy and unkempt.

Occupation? That was a tough one. He had been either too many things or too few to add up to something you could write in the space on a printed form. Not that he hadn't been occupied. Handyman, he said. He'd done enough of carpentry, wiring, plumbing, to qualify. He couldn't make out what the deputy wrote down. Bum, maybe; vagabond, derelict, good-for-nothing. Vagrant. At the moment, nothing else could be his occupation.

Fingerprints. Right thumb, right hand. Left thumb, left hand. No two sets alike, it occurred to him—like snowflakes. He stared at the mark of his uniqueness. A man was his fingerprint.

The deputy beckoned him down the corridor to the lockup, held open the door of the cell and then shut him in with a clash of iron reverberating, working down his spine. Bunk, chair, open toilet—the comforts of home. He sat down on the bunk, his nostrils hit by the smell of disinfectant, powerful, yet somehow impure, as though tainted by the corpse of whatever it killed. For just beneath the overbearing smell another odor leaked in, faint but pervasive, a presence almost that could not be drowned out. The residue of occupancy, an odor of staleness, like dirty socks or dried sweat, but more like something that, deprived of light and air, had taken its last breath and given up the ghost.

Well, here I am, he thought, as if he had reached a destination. And the other, where was he? Probably carted off to a hospital somewhere—the man who had fallen among ruffians. And he saw the fellow again, a vivid presence. He was red—face red, hands red. A figure sitting on the curb of the street, dabbing at his face with a handkerchief—covered with paint, or so it looked. But then, it had flashed through his mind, why would anybody be covered with red paint? Blood, he thought, just as quickly; that's blood. And he was close enough now to see that the face was streaming with blood, and the hands and arms. The handkerchief that the fellow kept dabbing in a slow unhurried way was itself red, a piece of bright rag held up to the flow.

"My God, fella, what happened to you?" he said.

"Some guys jumped me. Beat me up. Six of 'em."

Nothing like a fair fight. "You can't sit here. Where do you live? Want me to call somebody?"

"Better call the cops."

He didn't much want to call the police. As with doctors and lawyers and hospital personnel and public officials in general, he was content to live and let live. But the case seemed pressing. He crossed the street to the pay phone and put in one of his dimes. If he'd had any sense, he'd have quietly disappeared after doing his little duty. But the fellow was beaten up pretty bad. By the time he got back, he had passed out and was lying on the street. So he stayed till the cops came. He told them what he knew, while a few bystanders milled around, soaking up the scene and waiting till the ambulance came with a fine wail of the siren. They would have to start asking him questions. Once they got on the trail, they kept it up till they had him treed: no job, no money, no place to go. So they hauled him in. Did they suspect him of having beaten up the fellow himself? He explained that he'd come to town trying to locate a relative. Looking for somebody to leech onto, he could hear them thinking; yeah, we know all about it. Actually, he had already been to the town from where his father had sent the letter but hadn't found him. They hauled him in.

"Say, man, what'd they grab you for?"

He looked over to the shape leaning against the bars of the cell across the corridor. "For being plain damn dumb."

"Join the club. Never trust a buddy. Remember that—rule of life. Don't even let a guy smoke in here. What a fleabag."

Here he was—among those nameless others who had bequeathed their presence, a part of that brotherhood that had stood on the wrong side of a barred window. The walls bore the marks of their presence. Names and dates, notches to mark off the days, drawings

of women with extraordinary breasts and thighs like columns and
explicit crotches—goddesses of waiting and boredom. Obscenities,
doodles, scribblings, even a bit of verse carefully boxed in. The
pencil had smudged a little, blurring some of the words, but he
could make them out:

> The five cards in the cradle
> Are the five cards dealt by fate
> You're in a game of poker
> And luck is an inside straight.

Except for a few dirty limericks, he hadn't been much for verse since
the fifth grade, when Mrs. Pennuel had made them memorize it and
recite it to the class. But it was mostly high-minded and instructive
and never stooped to anything so low as a poker game:

> Build thee more stately mansions,
> O my soul, as the swift seasons roll,

he dredged up from somewhere, unable for the life of him to think of
the next line—what you did when you found a place you liked, if you
ever did, that was clean and livable and not too high in the upkeep.
He had not gotten things too well by heart, having lost all interest in
scholarship when the teachers quit reading stories out loud and
letting the kids draw pictures with crayons. His mother had spent a
lot of words and useless grief trying to shame him with the fact that
she had always been at the top of her class in school. With slightly
more effect, she used to sit with her sewing to keep an eye on him
while he struggled through his homework and would thump him on
the head with her thimble when she saw his attention lag. Maybe if
she had thumped him harder, the thought occurred to him, circumstances would have thumped him less; for he'd maybe have learned
whatever it was that was supposed to do him some good. He read on,
squinting to make out the words:

> Sometimes a pair is winner,
> Sometimes a flush is not,
> And you'll lose all your singles
> If losing is your lot.

Good grief, he thought—sure for a moment that his father must have stood in that self-same cell. It could have been his voice speaking, except for the rhyme. Whoever it was must have fared just as badly at poker. A descendant of Wild Bill Hickok? Like his father? Was there something at the marrow of things, he wondered, that made a pair of aces and a pair of eights unlucky? Something you'd get shot in the back for holding? . . . At least James Butler Hickok was the sort of man you could feel bad about getting it. Which he'd started doing about the time he was nine years old. Yes indeed. Drama of the Old West, Part I:

THE TRUE SON OF WILD BILL HICKOK

or

Ladies, If You Have a Love-child, Lie a Little

Scene:

Salida, Colorado, on the banks of the old Arkansas.
White frame house with pillars holding up the front porch. A
swing on that porch. The noise of that swing as it goes back and
forth, not a squeak exactly, but a low-toned rake, a comfortable
sort of noise. Himself on the porch swing, listening:
  I tell you, boy, there was no finer man than Wild Bill, Hand-
  some and brave. . . .
The old man, his grandfather, talking—in his eighties now,
come down to Salida, Colorado, to fret out his last years—a
straight-backed, hawk-nosed old man, impatient of old age.
  When I was grown up some, I went round to all the men I
  could find who'd known him when he was marshall in Abilene
  and Hays City. See, looka here, this is his picture.
The boy looks at the picture, studies it:
  He looks kinda mean with that mustache.
His grandfather takes the picture, holds it out in front of him,
can't hold it steady because his hands shake.
  No, boy, he wasn't mean, nor wild. They called him Wild
  Bill, only he wasn't mean and ornery, not like the ruffians he
  was trying to take a little law and order to in them wild cow
  towns. He never killed a man but in self-defense.

The boy looks at the picture again to make sure.
His grandfather: Once three men set upon him at the same time
 and he shot his way out alive. You had to defend yourself in
 those days. Still do. (Little sharp laugh.) And you remember
 that—the manly art of self-defense. (Gives the boy a little

friendly poke in the chest.) And remember what you came from. Remember now that when Jack McCall shot him in the back not all his blood ran onto the ground. The blood that is flowing in your veins, just like the blood flowing in mine, is the blood of Wild Bill Hickok. . . .

The old man holding him by a look, as though he were hyp-notizing him.

       ENTER *a thin, long-faced, bony woman.*

Wild Bill Poppycock, you mean. That's the only stuff flowing around here. No blood neither—just hot wind.

They look up. His mother, having entered upon the scene un-noticed, stands in front of them, arms akimbo.

His grandfather: *What do you mean, daughter, coming sneak-ing up that-a-way? And what do you know about what I'm say-ing to the boy?*

His mother: *You ain't no more descended from Wild Bill Hickok than I am. I know all about that: Well, I s'pose your ma had to have somebody to lay it on to—ha! Well, she picked one all right. To take the edge off the disgrace.*

The old man stands up, red in the face, the veins in his forehead looking as though they will burst. The boy looks at his mother, then at his grandfather. His stomach hurts the way it did when he ate too much candy and junk at the carnival.

His grandfather: *Shame. How dare you say a thing like that to me? And here in front of the boy . . .*

His mother: *And shame on you, filling up his head with lies and tales—all kind of nonsense. Hard enough time I got as it is pounding some sense into him. What's going to happen to him in the world, the kind of stuff you're loading him up with?*

His grandfather (under his breath): *Bitch.*

His mother: *What? Yes, well, I know how it is. You never liked me from the beginning. Thought I wasn't good enough for that precious son of yours. Well, you don't have to like me much longer—that's how it is.*

Words flying back and forth as the lights fade, carrying both his grandfather and mother into the darkness. A single spot-light lingers momentarily on him, held for questioning:

??????? GRANDSON OF A NOTORIOUS LIAR
AND SON OF A BITCH ???????

•   •   •   •

They brought him a tray of food, recalling to him that he hadn't eaten yet that day.

"Don't look too close at them beans," the fellow across the corridor told him. "You might see something move."

"Well, I'm needing a little red meat."

"Haw, well, it'll put hair on your chest."

The beans were hard and sapless like they'd had to be unstuck from the bottom of the pot. There were potatoes and something else swimming around in the gravy. He ate it all, wiped round the plate with a piece of bread, and sat back content, though he knew that the flavors would keep him company the rest of the night. True, he'd eaten worse, but not much worse.

•   •   •   •

But his mother had to be wrong. For if his father didn't bear Wild Bill's blood, he certainly shared his fatality at poker. Not that there was any other resemblance between Wild Bill and his father, a slim, middling sort of man who'd lost most of his hair and gone slack in the gut by the time he was thirty and could only spend the rest of his life getting balder and slacker. The only thing he'd managed to hold onto was a knot of worry above his nose. For the things that belonged to him had a way of deserting him and the rest had a way of going against him. Penniless relatives and stray cats turned up at the door, starving hungry and howling for food; and small-time hoods smelled him out for a little protection money like rats after crumbs. Otherwise he might have done decently enough with the bar he ran there in Salida, Colorado, though his wife never liked to mention what it was that bought the victuals and paid the bills. She'd have been better pleased if he'd run a grocery or even a feed store or traveled around selling some gadget that lightened your chores.

When he thought of his father, he could sometimes hear his voice and remember something of his general shape; but he could but dimly see his face. Nor could he put his impressions together to form a picture of the man. Specifically he remembered the three signs of his father's presence those evenings he was home and it came time for the kids to go to bed. He and his sister would be making a ruckus, chasing each other around the house, teasing and throwing pillows. His father would clear his throat. That was the announcement that they'd better quit horsing around and do what they were told. Nobody would pay any heed. Next his father would rattle his newspaper. They'd keep on. But when he started knocking the ashes out of his pipe, they'd tear upstairs. He didn't know why. He didn't know what his father would have done if they hadn't. Perhaps they knew by instinct that they oughtn't face him with the crisis. For it was his mother that always gave them a hiding. She kept a switch and she knew how to use it.

So that what happened afterwards didn't fit in at all; and nobody could say what it was that got into his father the night of the poker game. He wasn't what you'd call a gambling man. Two or three times a month he'd play a game of nickel ante, his one diversion. So there was nothing new in that. It was true that Avery was a stranger in town, and maybe a sharp stranger, though he couldn't picture it. More than likely, Avery simply fell into something. But if he were actually looking for a way to make his fortune, Fate led him to the right place. Even so, that still didn't account for his father. Maybe his father didn't know what was happening to him, found himself in so deep he couldn't get out. Or maybe he'd thought he could track down the luck that was always giving him the slip. Or maybe he'd picked up the cards as though the next day didn't matter because he didn't want to think about the next day.

Or maybe it was just a kind of fatality. Maybe the moment you were born, somewhere else was born the man who'd do you the dirty—the Jack McCall who'd shoot you down: like the yolk and the white of an egg. No matter how far away he was, something must be that beckoned a man's destroyer. Then the thought came to him, How about if one created him? It was a puzzle.

In any case, he didn't know what had gone on in the back room of the bar. The only part of the drama he knew about came after the game, and perhaps that was the only part that mattered. Drama of the Old West, Part II:

THE ERRING SON OF WILD BILL HICKOK
or
When the Chips Are Down, Boys, Never Let a Female Get the Drop on You

Scene i:

Darkness. He wakes to find voices rising up, piercing sleep like knives. He is in bed. He lies listening:

You're crazy. Drunk or plain crazy. Keeping me up till all hours, worried to death you'd got yourself killed or something worse. And now you come telling me you've lost the place. You're drunk or crazy.

He strains to catch the answering voice, his father's— low but not blurred.

Yes, lost it.

His mother: You mean . . . you mean you'd gamble away our living? You'd risk that? . . .

His father: Risked it and lost it.

His mother: Fine, oh that's fine, and what are we supposed to do now? Turn us out into the street. And what do you want— me to walk the street now? I'd prob'ly get us a better living than you ever got.

His father: Hush up, Ella, you'll wake the kids.

His mother: Don't you be telling me when to shut my mouth. I don't care if I wake the dead. You snake in the grass, you crawling, low-bellied, lying, sneaking . . . I could kill you for this. Oh, I could kill you.

He gets up out of bed and quietly slips downstairs to the door-way of the living room. He blinks in the light.

His father: You never liked the place anyway.

His mother: Oh, so that's how it is. She doesn't like it, so the hell with it. So now what are you going to do, you yellow-bellied, slack-gutted flea-brain?

His father: I don't know yet.

His mother turns, rushes to the little cupboard just to the side of the fireplace and takes out the Colt Peacemaker his grandfather swore had belonged to Wild Bill Hickok himself.

     Get out. Get out.

His father: Don't wave that thing around—it's loaded.

He rushes in, throws himself down, and clings to his father's knees.

His mother: What are you doing up? Get yourself out of here. This is nothing to do with you. Go on, get, before I take the switch to you.

His father: Put that goddam thing away. But then I s'pose you want my blood too. Don't worry, I'm leaving in the morning.

His mother: We can get along without you—all you've ever done around here. Well, all I'm saying is you'd better get your traps and haul your dead ass out of here by noon and not a minute past.

His mother turns and goes out of the room, throws down a blanket and pillow into the middle of the floor.

     Now get on out. If you want to sleep, you can sleep on the front porch . . . (then noticing him). And you get on up to bed.

He goes back up to bed and lies there in the dark. He can't close his eyes. He lies there holding up the darkness with his eyeballs. Suppose his father could take hold of that Colt and go after the fellow who'd done him in. Then there wouldn't be any more trouble. But there is a question. He slides out of bed, opens the window, and climbs out onto the roof and shinnies down the pillar. His father lies curled up in the porch swing, his head turned toward the back. He squats down beside him.

     Pa, what happened, Pa? Did he cheat you?

His father turns over, peers at him in the dark.

     Did he cheat you, Pa?

His father leans over.

     No, boy, he won it fair and square. (A long pause.) Sometimes you. . . . There's something . . . and you got to. . . .

The light goes on inside the house. The sound of steps.
His father: Quick, now, get on back to bed before your ma
catches you out here.

Scene ii:

Carrying his suitcase down the sidewalk of the empty street at
half-past noon, his father rides out of town for the last time—
on the Greyhound.

•   •   •   •

It was a night without peace. He'd dropped off to sleep when the
door of the cell next to his clashed shut on a pair of drunks they'd
hauled in from somewhere. One got sick all over the floor and the
other kept yelling for somebody to come and clean it up. Nobody
came. The smell was enough to unlatch his innards, and though he
tried to escape into sleep, the smell kept pulling him back.

They let him out the next morning after breakfast.

Sunlight took him by surprise, so accustomed had he become to
the glare of artificial light, which had its own kind of dimness. But
when his eyes were used to the sunlight and he'd filled his lungs with
air, he felt good all of a sudden, as though air and sun alone were
cause for celebration. Which direction now—north, south, east,
west? He had one more place to look before he called it quits and
moved on. He was almost afraid to look further, afraid the old man
was dead or else lying in an alley somewhere curled up next to an
empty bottle of rotgut. The one place he still had to look was the
fairgrounds. He'd come upon an old fellow in a grocery store/filling
station who seemed to know everything that had happened in those
parts for the last seventy-five years and who'd told him he
thought—yep, name sounds familiar—he knew a Hummer out at
the fairgrounds working in the carnival. And if it were his father,
what sort of thing would he be doing there?

Jason waited till nearly dark before he set out to answer the question, walking along the highway out to the fairgrounds, where all the
cars were headed, a lot of them jammed full of teenagers in a hurry.
He found it pleasant walking while the evening dimmed down to the

last streaks of sunset fading behind the hills. The air was cool with the lateness of summer, suggesting what would come: the kids starting back to school; the carnival packing up, the rides being taken down in great chunks of metal; the empty grounds left for the wind to pick at scraps of paper.

But there ahead, the sky was all livened up with strings and circles of lights, though it wasn't dark enough yet for them to stand out sharply. As he approached, he thought he smelled hot dogs. Food— and it smelled good. Since he wasn't about to pay for a ticket, he walked around till he found a place where he could slip into the carnival itself, in between the trucks that held the generating equipment.

He came in near where the ferris wheel was in motion to the grind and putt of the motor below. There were people on it, though not many, the empty seats rattling as they swung back and forth. Two girls flew shrieking past, clinging to each other as they went flying up, then down to catch the lights of the town in their laps. It might be, he considered, taking up possibilities, that his father was selling tickets for one of the rides or maybe peddling popcorn or candied apples, though he couldn't feature it.

He threaded his way through a crowd that was beginning to thicken up with ranchers and town folks with all their kids. Little kids yammering and pulling at the big folks to take them on the rides or buy them popcorn, and solemn staring-eyed babies kept up past their bedtime. He had to work his way around a bunch of the older kids laughing and talking, arms knotted, not looking out where they were going. A few of the gray-headed and thickset had plumped themselves down at the bingo game—a row of bottoms along a bench. The caller, with a voice that twanged like catgut, stood in the middle by a table piled up with lamps and waffle irons and sets of glasses and ashtrays on stands and black ceramic panthers, and called out the numbers.

Not at the ferris wheel or the bingo game, nor as a barker for the freak show, where the man with the rubber neck and the amazing man-woman were on display. Nor did he find him with the girlie show, where the girls stood out on the platform with set faces, like plaster casts, not giving anything away for nothing.

He paused a moment by the merry-go-round and breathed in the smell of hot dogs and popcorn and listened to the calliope and watched scenes of Indian maidens and swans, sailboats and islands with palm trees flash by. He'd wandered here and there without seeing anybody that bore the slightest resemblance to his father, but then he couldn't be sure he would recognize him after all these years. And the question occurred to him, What would he do if he did see him? All the time he had been looking, the question had never crossed his mind; only now when there was a real chance of finding him. For now he was convinced that his father would be working one of the booths. His father ought to know something about games of chance.

For the crowd it was a question of whether to throw darts at balloons or balls at weighted dummies, or toss rings around knife handles, or nickels at little squares; whether to pick a number that might come up at the spin of the wheel or place a coin on a horse in a miniature race—so as to win one of the great bright pink or blue pandas on the shelves or a cigarette lighter, pocketknife, or watch that glittered under the lights, but more likely one of the glass ashtrays hidden under the counter. He watched a young fellow throwing balls, three tosses for a quarter, while a girl waited for him to win one of the giant stuffed pandas for her. He had a pile of quarters on the counter and was determined to do it.

When Jason looked their way, the operators caught his eye, shouted to him to try his luck. "You wanna play, mister? You win some of these, eh?" The slang hammered out in a foreign accent made him pause to look at the face: high cheekbones, red hair cruelly dyed. But it was the voice that got him—hard beyond the hardness of things, but keen-edged with the sharper's interest in getting around them. She was turned sharper just like a man. A great screeching racket met his ears before he saw that the next booth was filled with cages of parakeets. "Come on, mister, ya get de boid." The flash of a gold tooth came with the laugh. Jason couldn't imagine his father among the sharpers, a crew that seemed to have come from an alien place, if not a foreign country. Some of them had served time, he knew. Nobody ever gave his right name if he was a carny, and if you were smart, you didn't ask.

Then he saw him, or at least he saw a man that could have started out as his father: an old man, nearly bald, wearing blue jeans and a checkered flannel shirt. The hair he had left was a shaggy fringe of gray above his ears and around his skull, and his belly was such that he had to belt his pants below it, two skinny little legs taking him the rest of the way to the ground. His care was half a dozen Shetland ponies rigged up to a wheel to make them walk in a circle and saddled up for children to ride. He lifted up the children and set them in the saddles and guided their feet into the stirrups and set the little animals to plodding around in a ring. The ride over, he lifted the children down and turned them loose. Then he went around to the ponies in turn, patting each on the head, giving each a bite of the apple he'd taken out of the pocket of the coat lying across the railing. Then he hoisted up a new set of children. But he had no eyes for the children, nor for their folks, who stood smiling and calling and waving to the tots in the ring. He had to get done with them to have his turn with the ponies.

As Jason watched, it came to him quite without premeditation that he would never go up to his father, even if he were positive it was he, and make himself known. For his father was no more linked to the past that included him than was one of the horses: he was a man alone, without wife or child or any other kin. It seemed that he might as well have forsaken humankind altogether and gone to the wilderness to live among mavericks, listening to coyotes and following the track of the wild mustang. But he had affection for the little horses, stroking their heads, giving each a bite of apple, a lump of sugar.

Uncertain for a moment where he ought to head, Jason stepped back into the crowd and drifted on past to the end of the midway. So this is what it all adds up to, he thought, turning to walk down the other side. Losing game or ace in the hole? The manly art of self-defense? He had a mental image of his father taking up the pack of cards and tossing them into the air, as though casting them into the teeth of fate, in that moment of risking everything and losing everything—to win back himself. He stopped for a moment, feeling slightly dizzy, the way he had felt that morning when he came out of jail. He wanted to laugh and he could have wept, and he could not tell an old ache from a new sort of awe, now that he had come and received his father's blessing: "You're all on your lonesome, boy. You're all on your own."

Decline and Fall

The world was coming apart at the seams. That much was clear. Any sensible person would drop what he was doing and rush to its aid before disasters dropped from the sky and the towers of earth were shot through with flames. But when had people ever been sensible? Evvie Skyler wanted to know. God Himself had perhaps been slightly off tilt when He made the Creation, forgive her for saying so. But a certain insanity seemed to have come with the world from the very first—even the axis inclined at a crazy angle, to allow for winter in certain climes. As if winter and snow and sore throats and doctor bills and endless worry over the furnace were absolute requirements. . . . She was reminded of the engineer who had laid out the town while under the influence. One of the streets had a crook in it that had thrown off the whole pattern of the town ever since.

But the creation— The plants and animals—the syllables of existence—all the clicks and chuckles and grunts that had taken on living form: and for what reason? Wolves and hyenas and toads and snakes and salamanders; cockroaches and mosquitoes and the common pestiferous housefly. Not to mention dinosaurs and leviathans. Done almost as a sort of play, just as if, having gotten tipsy and taken a step off balance. . . . And then when the question was put to Him, He got huffy about it. Just the way her father always did. Count on a man to yell whenever you questioned what he was about. It was a form of masculine logic.

And there was no question but that the world, the whole delicate, much patched and heavily revised edition, was becoming unglued, unseamed, split and severed. Fragmented. She was tempted to go for the thesaurus. But THE BUCKETS. She remembered them just in time. She put away the letter she had been contemplating, and the thoughts that had flooded the contents of it out of her mind. No time even to think. She had to scoot for it up to the attic of the library.

Were it not for her—and people, she felt, should be aware of this—the rain would long ago have come through the ceiling and down on the books below. Think of the mess. A ruin, everything lost, dissolved back into primeval mud. Were it not for her, she insisted, there would be no library.

Ramon never remembered the buckets. No matter how many times you got after him, it was like rain on a duck's back. No, he would stand there in great humility, quite like a schoolboy being chastised, while she vented her indignation. "Ramon, if the buckets overflow, all will be lost. Why can't you THINK?"

"Ah, Mrs."—he could never be made to comprehend that she had no husband—"I have been sweeping. . . . Forgive me, I am so sorry." He had a peculiar line that ran in under the lip and cut his chin in two, and it disconcerted her to watch the progress of that line through his contrition.

When she thought about the Mexicans in the town, she was always terribly sorry for them. They were such children, all of them—not sensible in the least. The little girls getting married when they were but children themselves, having babies, losing their bloom and fading out: fat old women by the time they were thirty, living in shacks with color TVs inside and big Buicks and Pontiacs outside, where their ragged children played in the dirt streets. They didn't know any better, so you couldn't blame them. But like children, they were exasperating.

". . . I have all the sweeping in all the buildings. . . ."

"Do you have children, Ramon?"

How white his teeth shone against the dark skin of his face. The line traveled up to divide his cheeks. "Ah, yes. Six children, Mrs."

Six children on a janitor's salary, and grinning to boot.

But it was she who had to take care of the roof. It was a sieve. She had telephoned the mayor dozens of times, from the day she had noticed the first leak—the water had come dripping down through a crack right above the checkout desk— till now, when the leaks were multiplied. They had sent someone over to patch the roof. But no matter how many patches they put on, they never quite got the place where it was leaking; or else, for every patch they put on, a new leak sprang into existence. They didn't want to put on a new roof, for they planned, at some vague and distant time in the future, to build a new library. From their point of view, there was no point in putting any money into the old building. But whether it would last till that hoped-for time in the future was something the city fathers didn't burden their minds with overmuch. Evvie Skyler, on the other hand, had to live with the situation. And her fears were that the floor would give way even sooner than the roof. How the boards creaked whenever anyone set foot on them! Not only that, one could see through the cracks between them into the basement. She suspected Ramon of sweeping the dirt down through the cracks instead of picking it up.

Nor were these all of her worries. She could not even leave the library in peace because of the park benches. At least, now that it was raining, no one would be sitting on the park benches.

She had called the mayor again that morning to have them removed. She was quite terrified to go home alone after dark on account of the park benches. They invited people to loiter, strange people who ought to have been elsewhere and who brooded up mischief in their minds. She had read accounts in the papers of women assaulted at night on their way home. But her objections extended to the daylight as well. During the afternoons after school let out, the high school kids were all over the benches. Heedlessly, they trampled the grass. She herself had picked up their empty coke cans and candy wrappers. Think of it—candy wrappers in among the tea roses in the flower bed planted by the Sorosis. The park benches had to go. She thought of how dark it was near the benches. The streetlight on the corner left but a solitary circle of light. You could scarcely see who was sitting there in the dark. . . .

Fortunately, the buckets had not overflowed. As she stood in the attic listening, it seemed as though the rain were letting up.

She found only one person in the library when she came back down, a slender, rather eager-looking young man with a bad complexion, who stood waiting patiently by the desk.

"I like history," the young man said. "I just read *The Rise and Fall of the Third Reich,* and I found that very interesting. Could you recommend something else on that order."

She brightened. "Oh, yes," she said. "If you're really interested in that sort of thing, you might try Gibbon's *Decline and Fall of the Roman Empire.*"

For a moment he looked puzzled. Then he thanked her profusely and left. It was a hopeful sign, she thought, when the young wished to improve their minds. So often they didn't. They wanted to read about Russian spies and rockets and motorcycles and getting rich. They cared nothing for where they came from or where they might be going. She was afraid their minds would atrophy and turn into unused organs, like the appendix, or even disappear entirely, like the tail.

Suddenly she was quite weary and, she had to confess, a bit agitated. The roof and the park benches. The letter coming as it had, breaking right in on her like an intruder, wrecking what little peace she had. . . . She had carried it around trying to think what to do about it, not reaching any conclusion. If she could but throw it away and be rid of it, but there was something insistent about a voice from out of the past, especially when it was about to materialize into a person in the present. It exhausted her to think about it.

After the young man had left, she went back into the office to take a nap before the grade-schoolers descended upon her. If anyone came in, there was a little bell on the desk for them to ring. When she was summoned from sleep, she always explained that she had been busy cataloging. It was, she had come to call it, a forked white lie. For she not only was not cataloging, she had never given herself the trouble of learning how to do it. In such a small library, it was scarcely worth the bother. She had applied her own system instead, quite workable. All the fiction was alphabetized by author and the non-fiction arranged by subject as well. Beyond that, she knew the location of every book in the library.

So that the townspeople thought her quite a jewel. Ask her about anything and she would say, "Oh, yes, you want the so-and-so," and lead you at once to its exact location on the shelf. "Whatever will they do when she retires?" some of the older ladies wondered among themselves. "She's an absolute marvel." Their good opinion, which, by extension, their husbands also shared, was the base on which she stood.

For she ran the library virtually singlehandedly. During the evening hours three times a week, a young woman came in to relieve her. She always took pains to hire someone docile enough to learn her way of doing things. There were requirements now for librarians: they had to pass the state library boards. Fortunately, she was exempt. But she was afraid that one day the town would want to hire one of those professional young persons who would insist upon rearranging everything. Up till now, the town being so small and the pay so meager, no one had stepped forward to challenge her position.

But the worry was always in the back of her mind, even though hers was still a name to be reckoned with in the town. Descendant of a pioneer family, her father had been the first doctor there. The local theater and the park had been named after him. Her father had used his influence to put her there in the library, and there she intended to stay, "until I become a relic myself," as she put it. A certain pride came with her humor. For she had a sense of history. Her grandmother had been in the West early enough to know the threat of the Kiowas and the precariousness of existence. The furniture and utensils Evvie had inherited had been at one time small claims made for civilization in a barren land.

She lay back on the black leather couch in her office, just above her the old pendulum clock that used to hang in the schoolroom where she had once taught. The ticking fused with the light patter of rain on the window. "I like history," the young man had said. Rare in the young.

At one time she had started a historical society for the town, inviting all those who had bits and pieces of the past to put them on display. For a time, there had been rather a nice little collection kept in one of the smaller meeting rooms in the library. She had been rewarded for her efforts. Knowing of her interest, a young rancher

came and told her about an Indian burial mound he had discovered
on his land. He had led her to it. And very carefully, without telling
another soul, she brought wonderful things to light: turquoises of
rich color and clay figures and pots with splendid designs. Not until
afterwards did she realize why she had kept her discoveries secret—
it was that she intended for them to remain so. She hoarded away
the treasure for safekeeping. That was all she wanted to do—just
keep it safe, safe for history.

And other things, too, that people brought in. She knew that they
could never appreciate what the old lamps and candlestick holders
and pitcher sets and knives and powderhorns really meant. Neglect,
loss, carelessness would take them from the human sphere. So one
by one she had slipped away the most valuable items of the collection, taken them home to lie in her own locked room. When their
owners appeared and asked for them back, she acted greatly upset,
blaming now the assistant who had moved away or the previous
janitor, who had had to be fired. One could never trust the Mexicans. People no longer brought in their treasures for the historical
society to display. A few dusty relics remained in the glass cases—
arrowheads and chards of pottery and some old prospecting tools.
An ancient stuffed owl, rather moth-eaten, kept watch over the
collection.

She herself remained above suspicion. For, after all, she had not
stolen anything. She was merely a custodian of the past, a guardian
of the treasure she could preserve better than the owners. Long after
she was gone, it would be there, a gift to future generations. No, she
had not stolen anything. Not for nothing had her father put her
there. She had simply held onto her mission in life.

She knew everything—all the life and death that had gone on in
the town. And all its secrets. She knew about the Treasury Depart-
ment man who had been found dead in a ditch one night during
Prohibition. And she could guess who might have killed him. And
she knew about the fire chief who had been sent to prison for bootlegging. And who should have been sent in his place. And she knew
about the school superintendent who had been married to many
women and who was divorcing his fourth wife. And how he spent his
time down in Juarez. She knew all these things.

The letter crinkled in her pocket as she turned over and made herself comfortable. She took it out and let it fall on the floor. Some things should never be allowed to erupt out of the past, she thought, and sighed and turned over again and, and as the ticking of the clock became the patter of the rain and both melted away, she fell into a doze.

While she slept, she had the sense of being awake. She dreamed that she had in her palm the thinnest, tiniest little old lady imaginable, frail as a leaf, and she was supposed to carry this fragile creature and not drop it. But somehow, careful though she tried to be, it fell out of her hand. And when she went to pick it up, it was as light and lifeless as a dessicated leaf or the abandoned shell of an insect. She awoke, disquieted. It was strange. The rain was falling harder; she must see about the buckets. She didn't want to get up. Something strange was happening. "Dear Evvie." The voice that she had trembled at when reading the letter seemed right there in the room. "Stay in the past, David," she said. "You've no right to come back." Once was enough.

II

"Suppose he doesn't like us," Bernice said, the usual challenge in her voice: what were they going to say to that? The three of them stood on the station platform waiting for the visitor who would arrive with his luggage of disapproval.

"You're being ridiculous," her father said—a habitual phrase. A heavyset man, portly rather, who carried himself as though he were much taller, he was accustomed to telling people what was wrong with them and prescribing what they'd better do for their own good.

"Suppose he finds us terribly *boring*," she said emphatically. "He's been everywhere and we've been—here. In this dull little town with dull little people."

"That's quite enough, young lady," her father said.

She subsided into silence, a certain set expression about her mouth that Evvie had come to recognize as a pout. It was a warm day and they were all perspiring, feeling their specially created appearances going a bit limp. The train was late.

Bernice always picked just such moments to be her most provoking. Evvie would gladly have shaken her. If only their mother had been alive. . . . Bernice was too old now at eighteen to be ordered about or chastised. But she was getting too headstrong for even her father to know what to do with her. Ever since he had taken her out of school—she had stood up in the middle of a class and defied a teacher—he had been quite at a loss. He had hoped to send her to normal school to earn a teaching license as Evvie had done. But Bernice absolutely refused to apologize to the teacher and go back to school. She wanted to go off to New York or San Francisco, to do exactly what she couldn't say. For a week she had worked as a clerk in an accountant's office; when the week was over she quit. Her father had been trying to bully her into making herself useful at home.

For the dozenth time Bernice went to the platform to see if the train was coming. She was bending far enough over to lose her balance—doing it on purpose, Evvie thought, for the sake of annoying them. The train would be there soon enough, and then they could see what they were in store for. Perhaps the young man would be a match for Bernice; he had certainly put his own father out of patience with him. In fact, they were to exercise their better influence upon him.

"See if you can talk some sense into him, Edward," Clyde Battelle had written his old friend. "I thought a couple of years abroad would take the foolishness out of him, but I see I was wrong."

"An artist?" her father had said, after he had read the letter. "Yes, I remember how Clyde would show off the boy's drawings when I used to visit. When he didn't think they meant anything." And he wondered that a rancher's boy in the middle of New Mexico would take it into his head to become an artist. In the midst of the Depression at that.

And from a good family, too, Evvie had thought, looking at the congressional letterhead. Written from Washington, typed by a secretary. But then, she remembered, a number of artists had come from good families. Toulouse-Lautrec, for one. But he had been unfortunate, indeed quite freakish, though of course he couldn't help it. And Van Gogh, who had started out as a minister. She had seen portraits of Van Gogh in books: the red unmanageable hair; eyes that looked at one with an intensity she found altogether unbearable. Mad, quite mad. And Gauguin, who had run away from a promising career and left his family to their fate.

To be an artist was to give way to those impulses that most decent people took care to keep under lock and key. Impulses that led to insanity at worst or sheer immorality at best. Or maybe it was the other way around. Which led her to wonder about David—how far gone he was in dissipation. Drink, idleness, loose women. The poor father, she had thought, before she ever laid eyes on the son.

As she waited with her father and sister on the platform, she couldn't help being in a stew. Was this the right sort of influence to have in the household? She felt afraid. Not for herself, of course. Now twenty-one, she'd learned from an early age to manage things, to be responsible. With two years of normal school behind her and a solid foundation in the classics, with the professional responsibility of teaching Latin in the high school and running the school library and sponsoring a Sunday-school class, Evvie foresaw no particular danger to herself. She feared for Bernice. Impressionable, wild in her ideas, unable to control her emotions. . . .

"It's coming," Bernice yelled excitedly.

Her father frowned. He did not like people to raise their voices.

"Twenty minutes late," he said, consulting his pocket watch.

They were able to greet Mrs. Emerson, who had been to Albuquerque to visit her mother, who was ailing; and Mr. Mercer, who had gone East on business; and then waited for the small assortment of people to descend from the train. Where was he? Not come, after all? What could have happened?

Then just as the conductor was calling for the departure, the young man appeared, a bit harried, large creases in his light blue summer suit.

"Are you David?" Bernice asked him immediately, drawing another frown from her father. How forward the girl was, Evvie thought.

"I fell asleep," he said, looking quite sheepish, no doubt embarrassed by his appearance. "I nearly missed the station." But for being a bit disheveled, he was quite an ordinary-looking young man. No red hair or wild look in the eyes.

"Dad sends his regards," he said, shaking hands with their father. "It's wonderfully kind of you to have me visit." And to the sisters: "I can't believe I'm in the West again. I feel that I've come home."

Evvie felt tremendous relief. Somewhere along the line, he had learned good manners. She glanced over at Bernice, who, after the initial excitement caused by his arrival, now seemed quite shy. And was very likely disappointed, Evvie thought. For he was not in the least shocking.

Because it had been so quiet a household, held up by the stanchions of school and church, the entrance of any stranger would have given a focus to their attention. Even the visiting Presbyterian minister, who had stayed with them earlier during the summer so that the Reverend Mr. Kemble might take his vacation, had excited a momentary flurry of interest. He was a kindly man, genuinely interested in their welfare, who said the grace at their table as though he would personally secure the blessings of heaven for them. After he learned that Evvie taught Latin, he continually brought in the scraps of his own education for her acknowledgment. He liked his coffee very sweet, and she could not help watching him put the lumps into his cup while she was trying her best to concentrate on what he was saying. One, two, three lumps into the cup. "And as the great Cicero [he pronounced it "Kikero"] would say, "O tempora, o mores!" Four, five, six lumps. "It was Cicero, was it not?"

Bernice treated him with such exaggerated courtesy that only a man as unsuspecting as Mr. Williams could fail to see the contempt it betrayed. Evvie was sure her father must notice it. But she dared not say anything to him about it. The shaky peace that existed between Bernice and her father was so shot through with his exasperation that the smallest thing could bring down his wrath. Any accommodation was better than that. In any event, the household took in Mr. Williams, closed over him, and was no better or different from what it had been before.

With David, it was otherwise.

"I'll be in and out a bit, if you don't mind," he said after they'd spent a weekend making him feel at home. "I feel the need to get back to work. What with coming back and being in Washington, I haven't done any work for a month."

"Come and go as you please," her father said. "We'll go on about our business. I'm in and out a good deal myself."

It could not be said that he disturbed the order of the household or imposed upon it. If he were there, he followed its routine. But he carried on another kind of life that was entirely his own. Since it grew out of his own personality, it had its impact on them. Because his own way of living transcended their routines by pretty much ignoring them, because he seemed to stake out an entirely different territory, he never ceased to draw the two women to him. They wanted to know where he was going and what he was doing. They found it impossible to curb their curiosity. They were ready to devour him—his knowledge, his tastes, his attitudes, as though in some way they wanted to be him, to see the world with his eyes.

His absence called attention to itself, because their imaginations took hold of it and filled it up; his presence drew them from their own activities. And though Evvie and Bernice, by reason of temperament, had never been close as sisters, yet with David they had a common ground. "Do you know what David told me today. . . ." And suddenly they had things to tell one another.

Often he was up and out of the house before it was light. Wearing denims and boots like any ranch hand, taking a sandwich and fruit, he went off to draw or paint, not appearing again until suppertime. Other days he slept till noon and worked until late in the night. His life had its own unique rhythms that did not consult the clock. He worked in sudden bursts of energy that took him out of their way for days on end. Then the work would be finished and, exhausted but exhilarated, he was ready to glut himself with their company.

The energy, the intensity that went into whatever he did seemed to awaken in them an unknown hunger. "Where did you go today?" they would ask him at supper. "Out towards Tenaja. There's a stretch of land there. . . . The clouds were great. I've never seen such light." Or "I caught a ride over to Trinidad and had a look at the town. Lot of people on the streets. The men stand around the city hall, sit on the steps—old men, miners, Mexicans. Good faces. I made some sketches."

A sudden discontent came to Evvie, almost as though she were envious of his experience. She found herself watching out for him, striking up little chats just as he was about to leave the house: "And where are you bound for today?" Bernice was on to her. On one occasion when Evvie was detaining him, she hung about so obviously that Evvie was embarrassed for them both. Smiling, he must have seen right through them. For he said, "Would you like to come with me?"

As though they had received a blessing, they made preparations for the day and went with him to the high meadows of Johnson Mesa. They drove out from the town, left the car midway up the mesa, and climbed the last three or four miles. When they reached the top, the world opened up around and beneath them, the deep blue of the nearer Folsom range on their right and peak upon peak of mountains in the distance below to their left. In front of them, the timothy grass rolled away in waves dotted with flowers. While David worked, they wandered through the fields in rich freedom. A hawk soared above them. They gathered wild flowers and returned to where David was painting.

After she looked at his canvas, Evvie wondered why he had troubled to climb all the way up to the top of the mesa. She looked in the direction from which he appeared to be drawing his inspiration, but she could not connect what she saw with what appeared in paint: a play of dark and light on shapes that were at once familiar and strange, formidable and even frightening.

"What's that?" Bernice demanded.

"What I see," he said.

"But what are you trying to paint?"

"Myself."

He wasn't joking, Evvie could tell, but she didn't ask what he meant. She didn't want to seem ignorant and give him a triumph over her. Some people enjoyed mystifying one, and it seemed wrong to give them encouragement. Perhaps it was wrong to accuse him of that. She would simply take from him what she could.

He was interested in the town as well, the town they had grown so accustomed to, they did not see it any longer. Their annual excursion to Denver to buy dresses was a reward for doing their duty by it. Somewhat dull on the one hand, extremely raw on the other, for it was a coal-mining town and a railroad junction, it was home. Bernice chafed under its restraints and privations; Evvie was reconciled to them. But David talked about the store that sold Indian jewelry as though it were a discovery, described the cheeses and salamis that the Italian miners bought in the little Italian grocery as though they were delicacies, and compelled them to view the old Greek who ran the candy store and made his own confections as a rare and wonderful being.

If he walked with them, he continually called their attention to things: to the way a cat was sneaking along a ledge after a bird, to the way the clouds cast their shadows on the hills below, to shapes and colors and expressions. His eyes took him everywhere, bound him to the earth in all its aspects, and brought him his daily adventures.

Because of him, their lives took on different shapes and colors. They came to depend on him in certain ways, and their relationships coalesced about their particular needs. To Bernice, who clamored for his attention, he gave a cheerful, almost rowdy fellowship, as with a younger sister, inventing things for her to do, teasing her out of her frequent moods of ill temper. For Evvie, his companionship was enough.

They spent a great deal of time together, to the point where her friends commented to her about it. And she would look about uneasily as they walked, wondering who might see them. And then, deep in conversation, she would forget to worry. What didn't they talk about? Books—the modern literature. Had she read any of Lawrence, whom he particularly admired? His experiences in Belgium and France, where he had gone to school. The Italian countryside, where he had gone on holiday. London theater. His work. And he had all kinds of questions to ask her, refusing to accept her verdict that her own experiences were quite insignificant.

Once she had asked him why of all the places he had been, he had come back to New Mexico.

"What more could you ask?" he said. "You know what Lawrence said about New Mexico? That there was only one other landscape equal to it—and that was Greece."

She'd always lived there in the mountains. They were part of what she looked out and saw every day. And then she went about her work. They were there, a setting for what she did, that was all—just as the town was. But David spoke of vastness and power and intensity. He spoke of vision. He sought out places she had given a certain meaning to and put by. Once he took her through the section of the town where the Mexicans lived. Dirt streets, yards filled with weeds and sunflowers and old crates and laundry tubs and various refuse, chickens and dogs wandering through. Dirty, half-naked children darted about, playing at some sort of game, chattering to one another in Spanish. One little girl was dragging along a younger brother who had no diapers or underpants on at all.

Evvie thought of the nurse who had told her how one of the women had tried to stop nursing and dry up the milk by putting turpentine on her breasts. Even though Evvie was a teacher, she wondered what could be done about such ignorance. David's head was full of romantic notions. As her father said, he didn't have his feet on the ground.

"When you're in a land like this, you need the things that make life go on. Do you know what the statistics are for TB in this state? Especially among the Mexicans? Do you know how many children die from malnutrition? Or in an area like this, the incidence of black lung? You've seen the filth and the poverty."

"So you think I'm wasting my time?" David said. "And being irresponsible to boot?"

"You can't live on air," her father said.

"What brought your people here?" David wanted to know. "Didn't they have a vision of the future and what the future might bring? Didn't they try to bring into existence something that wasn't there before—a dream? In my way, that's what I try to do."

"Nonsense," her father said. "They were starving miners hungry for land."

"Even that took a certain imagination," David said. "Lawrence's father never made it to New Mexico. People live as though there were no other way."

The first time he kissed her, she was entirely confused. He had put his hands on her waist and drawn her to him and put his mouth against hers. When his tongue brushed her lips, it seemed as though he would enter inside her and take away something she was afraid of losing. Flooded with sensation, her body was strange to her, and she felt ashamed. And if she didn't feel ashamed, she would lose hold and be carried away, as in a flood.

In an agony of confusion, she avoided him, pretended to be busy with other things. There were feelings she couldn't define, that fit into no definition she knew. Had he been a teacher or a lawyer or a businessman, she might have thought of marriage and home and family. But he had no real future, nothing she could visualize. If what she felt was love, where could it lead?

When she was alone with him again, it was even worse.

"I love you, Evvie," he told her. "Will you marry me?"

For one wild moment, she didn't know what to do. What could he possibly want from her? What could he possibly need her for? Then she said, "I couldn't."

"Why not?"

"It has nothing to do with you," she said, breathless with fear. He was inviting her, yes, to step over boundaries, put aside her family and her past life and leap into the unknown. She drew back her foot just in time. "It's impossible," she said. He has a wicked mustache, she thought suddenly, irrelevantly.

"Who's to stop you?" he demanded. "That is, if you love me."

"No one," she said, this time looking him straight in the eye. "No one but me."

He left them a few days later. He planned to spend some time on his father's ranch near Santa Fe, then strike out on his own.

III

She went for her purse in the office. Inside in the pocket was a handkerchief neatly folded, bearing her initials. For she had to weep.

Why had he done it?—her father—left nearly all he had to Bernice? All but the meager allowance that, together with her pitiful salary, gave her just enough to live on. Even though he had said to her after it was all over: "Well, you always were the sensible one, Evvie. No fear of you running off."

Indeed she had stayed, nursing him all through those last two dreadful years before his death from leukemia. At the same time their lives had been tainted by the scandal. She could not help blaming Bernice for what she had done—and David for permitting it. In one way or another, all of them had betrayed her.

She remembered how Bernice had moped around after David had left. There had been no living with her. Her nerves were high-tension wires. A mere word set her off into tears, into fits of temper. She had embarrassed them all by bursting into tears as David left. He had taken out his handkerchief so that she could wipe her eyes. And she had kept it. Wouldn't give it back. But no souvenir would suffice—it had to be all of him. A few days later they found her note— melodramatic, as was her style. She couldn't live without David. She would live with him whether or not he married her. Or die.

In the end, she did both—lived with him, and died, in childbirth. Too greedy for life—it had always been her trouble.

Evvie saw her only once before it happened. Bernice, pregnant, though she didn't tell Evvie so, came to make her peace with her father. Evvie had written her of his illness, and shortly afterward, she appeared. Whatever was said between Bernice and her father Evvie never knew, for neither of them spoke a word about it.

She came by the library briefly before she left. She stood by the checkout desk and talked to Evvie, not seeming to mind that people in the reading room could hear them. She and David were quite poor, but David was painting all the time. He hoped to get a show, maybe on the Coast. She had learned to cook. While Evvie was busy, she wandered restlessly about the reading room.

"Have you got a pair of scissors? she asked Evvie, as Evvie stamped books for two little girls.

Evvie reached into the drawer and handed her a pair. She watched Bernice saunter outside without thinking what she might be doing.

By the time Evvie went out to see what she was up to, Bernice had cut a sizable bouquet. "Lovely, aren't they?" she said of the tea roses planted by the Sorosis. "Those bitches owe me something."

And that was the last she saw of her.

The letter brought it all back, brought it once again to the point of pain. But a voice within her seemed to cry, "Redeem the past." Redeem it how? Where was the sin? Bernice had run off and died, so greedy for experience she had perished accordingly. And what had David done with his life? Painted pictures, it was true, but had ended up with neither fame nor money—a failure. The only real job he'd ever had, teaching art in a college, he lost for refusing to sign the loyalty oath. And her father had given away what should have been hers, rewarding the prodigal, the miscreant.

What was she to do? The voice within her was insistent, as though she had a mission. All right, then, she would see him. Even forgive him and let the past bury its dead. She had cared for him at one time. Perhaps he could come again as a visitor in the house. She thought of how he used to go out in the mornings to paint. Perhaps it was not yet too late. If he worked at it, he could earn a living by his art and lead a useful life. There were pictures on the walls of banks and the offices of waiting rooms. One of the ladies of the Sorosis painted as a hobby. She had won prizes at the state fair and sold her pictures for as much as a hundred dollars apiece, and gave lessons on the side.

She would be good for him. Perhaps she could have exercised her influence in the past. She could have steadied him, given him an anchor, whereas Bernice and he had been two of a kind. Flighty, emotional, irresponsible—no doubt taken in by a certain mysterious glamor, the lure of the forbidden. Bernice had perished; she would have survived.

But now David himself, down on his luck, having gone from one thing to another, had been sobered by life—or so she imagined. She would extend her hand to him, lift him up to where he had been before. And he appeared before her vision as he had been, the look of rapt attention in his face as he lost himself in whatever he was seeing.

Once she had made that decision she felt lighter in spirit than she had felt for many days. She called up the mayor's office and won a promise that the roof would be attended to and that the park benches would be removed the next morning.

When she closed the library and locked it, it was dark outside. As soon as she descended the steps, she saw that the streetlight was out—someone must have thrown a rock at it. And she was quite certain that someone was sitting on the bench, for she saw a dark shadow, darker than the shadows of the bushes. Suddenly she had a vision of David coming back, coming before she told him to—into the present. She was filled with terror, for as the shadow moved, rose and approached, she knew what she would see: a figure dirty and disheveled, looking as though it had slept in the alleys of a dozen cities.

"Don't come any closer," she cried. "Who are you? Are you David?"

Drunk, dissolute, the man she saw had become everything she feared he would. He mustn't come near, mustn't try to take her hand or make any claims on her.

"Go away," she cried. For he was right in her path. She struck out at him and then she ran. As she cast one quick terrified glance behind her, she saw his shadow in the rose garden. She ran until she was breathless and the pain in her side cut her in two.

Ghosts

"So it bothers you," his brother said, looking at him, smiling as though he had the goods on him.

The smile rankled. When a younger brother, hardly more than a snot-nosed kid, smiled like that, you wanted to bust him one. "Listen," he said, "don't get any ideas. Nothing bothers Joe Gargotta."

That had not erased the smile. But his brother was no longer looking at him; he was smiling down at the tablecloth, playing with a matchbook—their own cover: Napoli in white letters across the top, white birds beneath, flying across a field of blue, clean as handkerchiefs. Napoli—but in the mountains of New Mexico. "I mean it bothers you seeing her knocked up that way."

That did it. He shot up with a jerk that nearly tipped over the chair.

"Hell, don't get sore," his brother said.

"What are you thinking?" he said, grabbing hold of Frank by the shirtfront. "C'mon, c'mon, spill it."

"Crissake," his brother said, in a startled tone. "Ever since she went by, you been acting like you got boils. What're you jumping me for?"

"Don't put the finger on me, okay? It isn't like you think. I mean, hell, it could've been six other guys."

Frank's lips shaped a soft whistle. "Maybe you been doing some things you ain't been telling me about."

"When I feel like telling somebody my business," he said,

throwing the chair aside, "I'll write a letter. I'm going out," he said, in a tone that meant that anybody who valued his life had better not ask where.

"She went into Mendoza's," Frank said, giving his beer some serious attention.

"Listen, wise guy . . . " but he didn't finish the threat.

His brother chortled behind his back.

He thought for an instant of starting off in the opposite direction and cutting back through the alley, just because he knew Frank would be watching him. But he might miss her, and he wasn't sure where she was staying. He felt all tight. It would have been an exquisite pleasure to bust Frank, just for having been around at the wrong moment. He and Frank had been sitting over a quiet beer before things opened up for the customers, when she came past, carrying her belly, round and ripe, like a burden. "What's the matter?" his brother had said. "You look like you seen a ghost." Then Frank saw too. He whistled softly. "A few things have changed," he said.

She had gone past without so much as looking in the window. As soon as he saw her, his heart leapt with the fear that she would look straight at him. And what was he so knotted up about? he wondered, angry that he should be. If it hadn't been him, he thought, striding across the street, making a car stop for him, it would have been another guy. Did it matter who was the first?

He crossed the street and passed the grocery, looking in. She was still there, standing in front of the counter, a few inches farther back than she could once have stood. He waited, reading the letters of a poster on the window of the cleaners next door, advertising a chili supper at the Methodist church. He saw her come out.

"Maria," he said. She looked at him for an instant, her eyes opening wide upon him, but giving no hint of recognition, and in the next instant she had turned her head and was walking away.

He caught up with her. "You been sick?" he said. "Uh, I mean, you ain't been around."

She said nothing, so he stepped in front of her to make her stop. "Look, I mean, no hard feelings—okay? I didn't know you were in trouble." He touched his tongue to his lips before he asked the question. "It was me, huh?"

She nodded. "I went back to my mother."

"Oh, your ma." Then what was she doing back here? To be a pain in the ass, that was what. "She okay?"

"Sick—" She gave a little twist of her hand, as though to suggest that things simply happened the way they happen. "Dead now."

"Oh," he said, at a loss. "Gee, that's a tough break." He had a sudden inspiration. "Listen, you need some cash?" He pulled out his wallet. Should he give her ten, twenty? He had a couple of hundred on him. His impulse was toward generosity—Frank could snicker all he wanted. "Here," he said, pulling out a wad.

She put her free hand behind her back.

"Come on. Come on."

But she kept her hand behind her back.

"Now look, don't give me that kind of stuff."

As though thinking better of it, she put out her hand and he put the money into it. Put it into her hand only to see the bills go fluttering like birds to the sidewalk. There was a little ripple of laughter, as he stood there, for a moment much too surprised to think about what she had done. And when, stooping on the sidewalk, picking up the money, he had burst out angrily, "All right. Get on your high horse. Have your brat in the street, that's the way you want it," he was talking to himself.

Let her go then, he decided. He had tried to do the right thing, give her more than she could get out of him by any means including blackmail, and now she could go blow. If she thought she could squeeze any more out of him, she could forget it. He was somebody in the town; just let him say one word and she'd be out of there but fast if she knew what was good for her. He should have known better than to take out after her.

Returning, he plunged from the blaze of the sunlit street into the cool dimness of the dining room, where indirect lighting toned down the colors and softened the edges, kept the forms but let go of the features, creating the shadowy posh. Two of the girls were setting tables, with red cloths that kept the food stains from showing up, and Bill, the bartender, was putting on his red jacket. The musicians had come, were setting up their stands, and one, whose round face glistened as though he were sweating music, was warming up on the sax.

Joe walked back to the office to open the safe and take out the cash for both the bar and dining room cash registers. But twice he lost count midway through a stack of bills. He would start counting and then suddenly his mind would go blank and the number had fled. In the pause, it was as though things had gone gray, and he felt weary. One way or another he was a fool—a fool to have done it, or else a fool to let it get him. If she had not been strange, if only she had been the common sort, he wouldn't have gone to the trouble with her in the first place. But something about her had baffled and tempted him. Not just her inexperience—she was very young, virginal, he knew that—but a quality she had that made her seem a being from another world.

She had come down out of the Sangre de Cristos, from one of the little mountain towns that went back to the Spaniards and still hung on—relics, so poor and isolated they were almost untouched by change. And though she had come from a village to a town, not a very big town at that, she was like a child. The traffic frightened her, though the town had but one stoplight. She didn't know how much things cost or how things worked. She was constantly astonished by what people ate or bought or did or wore.

Her nature was a puzzle to him—dark and wondering—full of sudden fears and passionate bursts of adoration. She was Catholic— he had been, too, as a boy. She also believed in ghosts and witches. Her mother, she insisted, had seen the ghost of their ancestor, a young Mexican who came north with Coronado in search of the Seven Cities and was killed during an attack on the Indians.

Though he scoffed at her tales of witches that turned into owls and fled into the night on dark wings and of church bells that rang by themselves, he was intrigued that anyone should believe such rubbish. His mother had told him such tales when he was a boy. He could see a woman heavy in black—even as a young woman she had worn black—who told stories of the old country, an Italy so remote and distant it hardly existed for him. And when she told stories of her grandmother, who had visions, and of a certain miraculous tree whose white blossoms would cure a woman of barrenness, she seemed to have her eye turned toward a place where he could not go.

All he caught was a sweetish, sickly smell, like that of rotting apples. For her tales belonged to an older life that was dead to him, no longer able to feed or nourish.

But the girl held her head as though she saw what no one else could see, listened to a voice no one else heard. And perhaps it was because he could not get hold of it or even get close to it, indeed because it eluded him so maddeningly that he could not leave her alone. "Stick around," he told her one night, after her shift was over and they were closing up. "I'll give you a ride home." He had not said to himself what he would do. A little pool of feeling that seethed below the surface of his thoughts he avoided, perhaps so as not to see what was in it. But after everyone had gone and the two of them were left in the darkened restaurant, he had called her back into the storeroom. And there in the middle of the sacks of flour and potatoes, her face questioning, then full of fear, he had stopped her cries and forced her, as though he might penetrate her mystery and take from her the puzzling, secret thing she had.

He got his way through the cash, but his head ached. Suddenly he wanted out—the place was stifling. Frank could hold things down. But getting away wasn't easy. After he'd set up the cash registers, he was waylaid by Dixie, who got paid for smiling at the customers and who stood shimmering in a dress with some kind of metallic fringe that kept up a perpetual quiver. She had to tell him all about how, last night, a drunken bum had pawed and slobbered over her, insisting that only she could serve him his drinks. "Now you be sweet to me," he had told her, taking out his wallet and setting it on the table, "and you'll get some of that." And it was true she had gotten her share all right, the drunken pig.

"Well, keep the customers happy," he told her; that was what she got paid for.

"Yeah," she said. "Big joke."

His head was killing him, so he escaped to the kitchen to get away from her. But he might as well have stepped into the middle of a dogfight. Jimmy and his Aunt Lena were at each other's throats again. It took only one extra cook to make him tear his hair, to say nothing about spoiling the stew.

Every night when his Aunt Lena carried her bulk into the kitchen, his cook, Jimmy Gonzales, did a slow burn. He didn't blame Jimmy. His aunt was sure the restaurant would collapse without the pot of meatballs and spaghetti sauce she fussed over, tasting and seasoning. All right, let her think so, if it made her happy. They could even overlook it when she got in everybody's way, if only she didn't have to rule the roost besides, bossing Jimmy, nagging the girls if they didn't pick up their feet fast enough to suit her.

Tonight it was the same old story.

"Yeah, yeah, we know all about it," Jimmy was saying. "We know you're the only one in here knows how to cook. Me, I'm here only to look at the girls."

One of the girls laughed.

"What- what- what you say?" The old woman turned on him angrily, as though she suspected an insult even without hearing it.

"What's going on here?" Joe said. He knew what would happen. Jimmy would blow off steam; his aunt would go red in the face, stammering because the words for her outrage were hard for her to get hold of in English. Then Jimmy would grit his teeth and tell her he was sorry, in a tone of voice that would have made a slap in the face easier to take. But it would do. The air would be cleared, and things would go on as usual. But tonight, maybe because he was tired, jumpy, he would have been happy to knock their heads together.

"She just comes to make trouble," Jimmy said, "to get in my way, when I got trouble enough. Look, I do all the ordering, I do everything in the kitchen to save money for you. You tell me in the kitchen I am the boss. She comes in . . . do this . . . do that . . . we don't need her to be boss too."

"Don't need," the old woman said. "And what you do without I make the spaghetti. They order the chicken, they want with the spaghetti. They order the steak, they ask for the spaghetti. Everything—they ask for the spaghetti."

"Spaghetti? You call that stuff spaghetti?" Jimmy said, more than loud enough for her to hear. "It's no good. I can cook the spaghetti," he said, tapping his chest.

"No good!" she shrieked.

"No good," he repeated. "And you know what the customers say?" he asked her, leaning toward her as though telling her a secret, his eyes widening, bugging out. "They say it's like little mealy worms."

"What you say? Worms? My spaghetti?" She was nearly choked with fury.

"Look," Jimmy said to Joe, "you hire me to run the kitchen, right? Now I run the kitchen or you get somebody else, right?"

"Okay, okay," he said, and ran his hand across his forehead. If his cook walked out of the kitchen, he was in a hell of a fix. "So you got the spaghetti," he told his aunt. "Let Jimmy get to work. Go on home." He waved his hand as though he were waving off a fly.

But she stopped and looked at him, and he saw the tears spring to her eyes. "Joe, how you treat me," she said, and turned to go.

"Oh, my God," he thought. And he walked her to the door, trying to soothe her while she wept into her handkerchief. "Worms. My spaghetti like worms," she wept. Goddam women, he thought. Every time you turned around, they gave you trouble. He'd let things go too far. They did not need her to cook the spaghetti. They put up with the old woman because of some deep-rooted insanity that Italians had carried from their boot-shaped country. And what it meant was that instead of shoving the old woman aside, you let her walk into the kitchen to cook her pot of spaghetti and give everybody a hard time. And why? For the same reason he didn't yell at his mother, even when he felt like it. But this time things had gone too far.

His aunt was still shedding tears when she left, despite his efforts to get her to turn off the water. He felt trapped. If the old woman came back, Jimmy would make his life miserable. And if she didn't come back, she would haunt him like an accusing spirit, always pointing a finger at him. To get her to return, he'd have to grit his teeth, go to her and beg her—that was what got him. The hell with it. As he walked back into the kitchen, where the air was thick with the smells of hot grease and chicken frying and spaghetti sauce and the leftover flavors of past dinners, it seemed as though all the odors came together as a single bad taste in his mouth he'd have been glad to spit out.

"Want something to eat?" Jimmy asked him.

"Hell, no," he said, with an impatient wave of his hand.

"What's eating him?" he heard Jimmy say, as he walked straight through the kitchen and out, letting the screen door clatter behind him.

He walked out back, breathing the cooler air, standing where the slope began downward and the land was empty. He listened for a moment, hearing a blend of voices behind him, a ripple of laughter—one of the girls—then the jittery sound of glasses being set down somewhere.

Where should he go? Down through the town—the town he had lived in since he was born? Walk past the bank and the stores and barbershops, owned by the sons of those who had come there—Italians and Yugoslavians, Welshmen and Yankees, who had come to live in the company towns once scattered through the area and to dig and die in the coal mines.

But a few of the hardier ones, his father among them, had wrestled with circumstances and in the end had taken what they wanted. When Prohibition came, his father saw his chance and made a good thing of it. He left his wife to fuss over the little grocery and dry-goods store, a losing business, that was to have been his stepping stone to Fortune. With the money that came from bootlegging he had bought land, continued to buy and sell until he died, a rich man. Now his sons owned half the town. Others, too, hardly able to speak a word of English when they first came, had grown rich, lived to see their children seize opportunity as well. Now they were all Americans, who had found their common destiny in this land, only their names reminding them that there had been a past, a different land once. And it had taken strength, courage for them to lay hands on what they wanted. For, as though just behind a curtain, were secrets that came like whispers out of the dark. Once, when Joe was a boy, the house had been alive with whispers, and even in the streets of the town something spoke, something lurked. A Treasury agent found dead in a ditch. People talked, but that was all, and went on bootlegging whiskey and selling shoes and bread.

He started off into the grass, where the crickets chirred, and walked down beyond the reach of the voices behind him. The sun was setting, leaving an afterglow on the slopes of Eagle Tail and Tenaja, the land beyond them a smooth tan hide in the distance. Mountains, he thought, as though he were surprised they were there, and watched as the light concentrated in a final blaze as the sun went down. It was as though it had just now occurred to him that the mountains were there even when he wasn't looking at them, a presence, forming part of the landscape. A sudden rustle in the grass startled him, and he looked in time to see a horny toad scurrying into the brush. Ugly things. They should have eaten each other up with the dinosaurs. The mountains, he thought, had been there a long time. He thought of Indians and arrowheads. The Spaniards had brought horses. His father had brought guts. Now he. . . .

Maybe it wouldn't be such a bad thing, after all, to have a son. He'd gotten his loot, had had his share of good times off it too. Even now, at forty-six, with an eye toward a few more of them, he didn't want to tie himself down. But then, it would be a good thing to have a son to take up where he left off, to carry things forward into the future. It struck him funny: just when he'd been suffering because some chick had put the screws into him, he had to think it was a good deal after all.

Now he thought of the child. He must see that Maria got into the hospital so that his boy would not be born in some stinking hovel, in the filth and dirt. His memory turned up the one-room shack of rough adobe he had taken Maria to that night almost nine months ago. And he had a sudden horror of the child being born there, coming into the world naked, with nothing to cover it after it got there.

He leapt up quickly and left the slope of the hill, as though what he had to do could not wait. It was late, the stores were closed, but his mother's place would still be open, for the sake of her cronies, the few old Italians who came to get their olive oil and provolone and stayed to gossip. He walked toward the old section of town, run down since the coal mines closed and the train yard declined. One could barely make out the letters on the sign above the door, "The Golden Rule and New York Store." But the bell still tinkled when the door opened.

He went in, found his mother as usual, perched on a high stool behind the counter, reading the evening paper. He went through the ritual of asking after her health and listening to the store of gossip and complaint she had worked up since the last time. Then he wandered to the back of the store and began rummaging among the dusty shelves. His mother had not sold a piece of clothing for years, nor had she discarded any of the old unsold merchandise. High-button shoes and bowler hats were still piled up on the tables. Now and then theatrical companies bought some of the old stuff.

"What are you looking for, Joe?" she said, coming back to where he was. "What you want?"

"A blanket," he said. "You got any blankets?"

"Not since a long time."

"I need one." He didn't want to say more, but he couldn't avoid it. "Maybe you got a baby blanket, huh? Maybe something you had around."

Her face lit up. "Wait."

He waited and fidgeted while she went back into the rooms where she now lived alone. When she came out, she held out a small blue blanket, folded. "Yours," she said. "I kept it." She looked at him, smiling as though she expected him to be surprised.

He shook it open. "But it's falling apart," he said, vexed.

"It was yours," she said. "I kept it for all this time."

It was all in holes, the moths had been at it. His kid ought to have the best, he thought, and if the stores were open. . . .

"It's gotta be a new one. Well, see you later." And he rushed off before she could pester him with questions.

Now he had to find Maria. He was sure she'd be staying in the same place, with the old woman she had lived with before, but he was not sure he could find his way back again. He crossed the bridge over into the Mexican section, leaving the paved street and going along the dirt lanes that ran with water when it rained. Not a paved street in the whole section, not even in front of the whorehouse, which property he owned. They could find their way to it without a sidewalk, that was for sure. A dog barked at him as he turned into another lane between the adobe huts. It was at the top of the hill, he remembered, and when he got there, some old metal tubs in the yard looked familiar. He knocked at the door. The old woman came.

She opened the door and he could see past her where Maria lay on a wooden bed with a Mexican blanket thrown over it. "Don't let him come in," she cried. "Why does he come here?"

"She should go to a hospital," he said, in a low voice to the old woman. "I'll pay," he insisted, taking out his wallet.

"Wait," she said, and closed the door.

In a moment she was back. "She don't want nothing. She don't want to see you."

"But I am the baby's father," he protested.

"No, no," the girl cried. "He's not the father. It is not possible."

He was thrown off balance. Not the father, she said. Could it be true? Then he was right about her—he was not the first. And yet before. . . . But then, he thought, with a great whelming of relief, she wasn't putting any claims on him. In fact, she denied all claims. He hadn't done anything after all.

"All right," he said to the old woman and put his wallet back into his pocket.

When the door had closed at his back, he stood for a moment on the edge of the hill. There was the land, the hills nearby covered with tawny grass, those in the distance taking on the blues and purples of approaching night. He heard a whisper in the dry grass, listened and heard it again. But there were no ghosts whispering to him from out of the past; he was free. There was only the land, the land that belonged to those who seized it, possessed it, dug the mines, fenced it in, ran their cattle, sold them off, drank their booze, and didn't get out of the road for anybody.

His place must be jam-packed by now, he thought, and turned down the hill toward town.

Unraveling

The white rush of fury held dark imaginings. "I will tear," she avowed, "the eye from the eyeball." Crack it like an egg, drop yolk from white. And his teeth, she would count like beads into a little clickering pile. With the knife, ah the knife, she would carve in his midriff the initials of her true feeling. And from his belly pluck out the gizzard of this chicken, this buzzard. No, worse: this jackal, dog, hyena. Far worse: rat, louse, slug. Not even an insect deserved the comparison. Following at his heels along the darkened back street, where any figure was itself dark, bent, it must be, on concealment, she could find no name for the scruffy human with the itch in the flesh or whatever it was that tricked the blood. The blood itself would be made to answer. No name, but a cry, "Let Blood!" Take a knife to the very parts that had offended.

Perhaps she should have had a curved dagger, set with gems; a silver letter opener with an ivory handle; or some delicately mortal blade fashioned with great skill by the Chinese. It was an ordinary kitchen knife she had snatched up, a native of the hardware store. A countess, she should have borne a dagger. It would have been beneath her to use so lowly a weapon but that he deserved no better. A kitchen knife for the other, too. A slut. A waitress. One more piece of meat that belonged in the kitchen with the rest of the scraps. Except for what she had in front and the wiggle she had behind, that, under a tight skirt, lured a man's thoughts to the bedroom. Rosita. She was sure of it. She had sent her packing when she worked at the lodge, for twitching her butt at all the men. Now she had taken her tail to the hotel, and he had followed after. She was not worth killing. It would be enough to yank out her hair, scratch out her eyes.

When it was all over and everything came to light, she would be exposed, undone. Even with the fury singing in her blood, quickening shapes before her eyes, she knew. Suppose she could let it go, pretend to know nothing, act as though nothing had happened. Go home, drop the knife back into the drawer, where it would lie until the girls needed it to chop vegetables or cut up meat. Go to sleep, close her eyes to it. She'd rather be dead. She could as easily grovel at his feet or beat her breast before the town. And why was it, knowing what she pretended to, she could not turn away her eyes, but where the hidden and the vulgar revealed itself she must look?

The men, a bunch of dumb cowhands, had known what she now knew, and that morning she had read from their look the offhand contempt that belongs to boys ready to stomp an anthill—or to gods. She had wanted to smash their faces. Their smirk had curved over the morning. She had been unprepared for it: a morning that shed light on things, uncovered what had been hidden and exposed the strands of event beneath the outward surface. One seized hold of a thread and unraveled mysteries.

She had come down from the lodge breathless, ready to lash him with her tongue, and set out for the stable. He wasn't there, just the two hands, Lonnie and Burke, trying to repair a broken harness. They looked up when she appeared in the doorway, and in that moment of trying to force down her anger, the simple question in their faces of what she might be wanting now was enough to goad her into telling them what stupid sons-of-bitches they were. Ordinarily she did not set foot in the stable unless she wanted to ride. She sent her messages with one of the Mexican boys. A horse snorted and stamped.

"Where is the Count?" she demanded.

"He's not here, ma'am," Lonnie said.

"I can see that for myself" —stared at him until he looked away. "What I want to know is where he is." She hadn't found him in the lodge and he wasn't in the stable. The horses were still there, so he hadn't gone off on one of the trails with any of the guests. "Has he been here?"

"Well, not what you'd say a minute ago."

"And what would you say then? " she asked, in a honeyed voice that trickled sarcasm.

"It might've been five minutes ago," Burke drawled. "Then maybe it was ten minutes ago. But then agin, on the other hand, it might've been. . . . "

She cut him off. How dare he provoke her? "Did he go off with any of the guests?"

"It just might've been fifteen minutes ago."

Enraged, she turned to Lonnie.

"Can't say for sure, ma'am. Maybe he did and maybe he didn't. I mean, when I saw him, it looked like he was taking off for town." He wasn't looking at her, it was a good thing for him. A spot just above and beyond her right shoulder seemed to compel his attention.

The bastard hadn't told her where he was going or even that he was going. Turning her back on the men, she put her hand above her eyes, straining to see to the bottom of the hill. She couldn't see the truck parked under the cottonwoods down below. He must have taken the truck. When she turned back, she could sense that the two men had a bond of understanding between them. They had used that instant of her back being turned to swap a look.

"Do you *know* where he went?" she asked quietly, driving in the word like a spike.

"No, ma'am, I mean, Countess," Lonnie said, and went to fiddling with the piece of leather he was holding in his hands.

The insolence. They deserved a thrashing. She had to put them down. Whatever they knew gave them the edge, because she didn't know it. "It is of no consequence," she said, throwing the word at them, the ignoramuses, to look up in the dictionary. "I've business in town myself. I'll catch up with him."

"You might just do that," Burke said.

"Saddle the horses," she commanded, telling him what he was

already in the midst of doing. "There's a party going out this morning.

Then she stalked out. Outside she had to get used to the brightness. Even so, her eyes did not make the accomodation altogether. There seemed to be a quirk or bend in the sunlight, as though something moved just beyond eyesight, something quick as laughter, and fell into the crevices beyond the turn of the eye and disappeared. Something scurried through the brush—a lizard, very likely, or a horny toad. As she walked down to the car, she heard laughter, behind-the-back laughter. And something turned over inside her. When you were somebody, there were always threats: they stood waiting, all of them, like a flock of kites ready to swoop down and feed on your guts.

She remembered the bills she was still holding in her hand, bills from two and three months before, that she thought had been paid. He was supposed to take care of all that. How could he have let them go? And some she couldn't account for: bills from Mimi's Dress Shop. She hadn't bought anything there since they had first come to town and were flashing around a bankroll. And most of her stuff had come from one of the best stores in Dallas: western shirts of brilliant silks and white leather skirts and black pants with silver studs along the sides, and tooled leather boots. And the bills, they had made certain, did not follow them when they skipped town. But here they had to be careful. What did he think he was doing? And then, she wondered, why had he kept all this from her? Even if she confronted him, what would he say? And she knew then that there was no one she could ask, him least of all.

Even so, she went to Mimi, who had sent the bills. She was the only other person she knew of in town besides herself who spoke with a foreign accent. Mexicans didn't count, nor, for that matter, did Mimi. For who was Mimi?

"Ah, Countess. So wonderful to see you." Mimi herself, shoving aside her clerk, came rushing forward. Though she appeared as if dressed for tea and wore her gray hair like an elegant wig, she was very short. Like a little gnome, the Countess thought. And she had thick swollen-looking ankles. Very ugly. "Oh, we have just had some luffly things to come in. You must look, you must try on." So gracious was her smile that the Countess wanted to pinch her. Her accent gave hints of Paris and Berlin and for the ugly backward mining town, squatting in the sagebrush, shaped the word "Fashion."

I know you, thought the Countess, catching the glint of shrewdness in her eye. Some neighborhood in Chicago or Detroit or New York had spawned her, where immigrants had clustered, gabbling in incomprehensible tongues, even down to the third generation. And the beautiful dresses she brought back from her buying trips to California: someone had found a cleaning tag in one of them.

"I am looking for a long dress—for a party," the Countess said, "something trés, trés elegante." I know you, she thought.

"Hilda—the ones that just came in," Mimi said to her clerk. Then to the Countess: "A size eight, is it not? So slender, so svelte. Size eight, Hilda. Quickly please."

She had even remembered her size. Clever of her. She watched Mimi, who started to say something, then appeared to change her mind. She bit her lip thoughtfully, smiled. The Countess smiled also. It appeared that they were both holding the ends of the same stick. Very likely Mimi wanted to know about the bills too, when she was going to get her money. If she held her tongue, Mimi would say something.

"And did the Countess like her present?" Mimi asked, while they waited for the clerk.

A present. Ah, she had come straight out with it. She looked into Mimi's eyes to see what Mimi knew. "I get so many," she said with a shrug.

"The Count is very generous."

She acknowledged the obvious by tipping her head slightly. "And which," she said in a bored tone, "were you thinking of?"

"The beautiful negligee he bought . . . oh, it has been a little while ago."

"But of course. How very stupid of me. Beautiful, yes." So it was a woman. It was what she might have expected of him.

"The Count likes lacy things," Mimi said archly.

"A very naughty man," the Countess said, looking disdainfully first at one gown, then another that the clerk had brought for her inspection.

She gave a little affected laugh in response to Mimi's. She wanted to spit. Want your money, don't you? she thought. She held up one of the gowns, looked at it, tossed it over the arm of the clerk.

"He was in this morning," the clerk said. "Oh, I hope I haven't given something away" —raising her hand to cover a little embarrassed titter, then showing a mouth full of long, uneven, bad teeth. Like roquefort cheese, the Countess thought. From her face, common as mud, the Countess could number the long years of devoted Sunday worship and the weekdays of being bullied by Mimi. Such people were born into the world to be spurned with a foot. She dismissed the gowns with a wave of her hand.

She saw Mimi frown. "And how was it I missed him? Ah, I must have been to the bank."

And how could Mimi have let him get away? A pity, she thought. And when would Mimi, with an "Oh, I am so sorry," cut off the Count's credit and start hounding him? But the frown had dissolved, and as she held the door open for her, Mimi winked at her. For an instant she caught the depth of those eyes that had looked the world over in their shrewdness and knew everything. And she feared that what they didn't know they could guess—about her, too, and could look down on her accordingly. She very nearly envied her. Mimi, with her small collection of shams, would get by in the world. Soon people would forget about the cleaning tag in the dress, and she could go back out to California and buy more dresses cast off by socialites and movie stars and sell them for new. If any were the wiser, they would not care, for they needed Mimi to sell them luffly things.

Thin pickings. She had demanded more of the world than Mimi had. She, too, had started out in such a place, a yardage shop where she was learning to do sewing for the ladies of the town. Hadn't everyone who started out at the bottom worked in such a place: in some five-and-dime or hardware store or clothing store or else in some two-bit corner restaurant, waiting on tired-out women with varicose veins who dragged along sticky-faced brats, or serving plates of grizzly, tepid food to paunchy men strong with sweat. Done it and yearned somehow to show them, to be somebody?

Old Lottie Spinaker had picked her up, an orphan, practically off the street. And she had gone them one better, the three sisters who had made such a good thing of their shop they could look down their noses at the rest of the town. For Clothilde had made a name sewing for years for the Hollywood studios, even, it was said, making dresses for Shirley Temple. So that when she left Los Angeles to go back to Pyrite, Colorado, she'd gone right into business with her two sisters. Natalie had put up the cash and Lottie handled the yard goods and Clothilde did the sewing. . . .

One day after she had been sewing all day on Lydia Tuttle's trousseau, she had a vision—a vision of the whole world coming into the shop and picking out their clothes and parading them across the stage in a fashion show. The rich chose silks and brocades and the poor chose rags; the victors chose red and the defeated chose black; the beautiful chose lace and the ugly chose sackcloth; the proud chose purple and the meek chose yellow. And everyone acted accordingly. For what they wore was what they were. All she had in the world were the dress she worked in, two pairs of Levi's and a hand-me-down from the judge's daughter to wear for Sunday good. And that put her in the way to sew up Lydia's trousseau and to spend the rest of her life chained to a sewing machine.

That night when the town was still, she sneaked down past Lottie snoring in her bed, rummaged around the shop and bundled up the dresses in Lydia's trousseau. She took them and the little bit of money she had saved up and set off for the bus station, not knowing where she was going but certain of one thing—that if you tricked yourself out smart enough, you could trick the world. And no doubt because she was looking for him, she found a man who wanted to be a count as much as she wanted to be a countess. For you might as well pick a place at the top. And what beautiful designs they had made on the fabric of things. Now, trailing him to the hotel where he was headed for a little romp, she was about to rip out the threads.

II

She was in a snit. "What do I want with these things?" she said, throwing down wrappings, box, and the pair of black lace panties they had enclosed. "This I have. Next time, bring me money."

"Rosita," he said, stroking her arm, trying to soothe. He leaned toward her on the bed, where he had been lying watching her undress. She performed for him, taking off her clothes piece by piece, as though her nakedness were a dazzling finale after an unveiling. His clothes lay on the back of the chair, but hers made a little trail over the room: her dress lay draped over the dressing table, her slip and stockings had fallen in a little heap on the floor. But she had paused, going no farther. She shook off his arm and continued to sit on the edge of the bed without looking at him. Even from the back, following the curve of her spine, the tapering of the waist and the curve into the hip, he liked to look at her. Body: curve into movement, movement into rhythm. He brought offerings, gifts, as though to give her flesh the fit apparel of his desire, the cunning design of threads in little flowers, the embroideries, the lace that revealed her sex even as it concealed it. He had bought negligees for her and panties and brassieres that made her body carry out his suggestions for it, of softness, of luxury—that made it a garden where he might enter and browse among the flowers. He took hold of her elbow to pull her toward him, but she snatched away her arm.

"Oh, little Rose, don't be angry," he said, amused by her changeableness. He wanted to laugh at her, the way one laughed at a kitten for getting its back up, spitting.

She turned to look at him. She excited him when her eyes flashed. "You think I'm joking," she said. "Money, do you hear?" —making the gesture of counting it.

"You don't think I've come through," he said, with a touch of humor, imitating her gesture. Though he liked to spend money, made free with it when he had it, just now he was strapped. The thought of money was a thorn in his side. The bills he had been running away from. . . . "Well, let me tell you, my little gold digger. . . ."

"This room— You want to come to a place like this?" she said, palms extended to take in the walls, the ceiling, everything around her.

What did she want, he wondered, for a little roll in the sheets? A hotel room didn't come for nothing, not to mention the little extra it took for the night clerk to keep his nose clean and his mouth shut.

"I want a place—a room, an apartment where you can come, where I can be ready to meet you. I want to wear nice things for you. . . . "

"You do okay, Rosie, I'm not asking for the Queen of Sheba." She was beginning to get on his nerves. What's with this little whore? he asked himself. All of a sudden she was going high-class.

"I want a place of my own," she insisted. "From work I go home." She wrinkled up her nose, as though she had caught a whiff of garbage. "Two rooms and all my brothers and sisters."

"Listen, sweetie. There's no place like home. Don't get too many ideas."

"It stinks," she said, stamping her foot.

"Listen," he said. "Let's keep it high-toned. We've had a good thing, you and I. A little fun—a few presents."

"You come to me. You like me to wear beautiful things. . . . "

All right, a man likes to dress up his kitten. But beyond a certain point. . . .

"You are a count," she said, getting up and facing him. "Very rich." She picked up his shirt from the chair and, putting it on, paraded about, as though dressed in robes.

He laughed. "Yes, never forget that I am a count and very rich." The world was full of counts and countesses, some well-heeled and some without a pot to pee in. They all had blood, and they all had birth. As if nobody else bled when he got stuck, as if no other female could claim that the brat she sent into the world was a noble son and heir. As for himself, he was a count by choice—no mere phony, but a consummate artist. Being a count was a profession like everything else. Everybody had to choose the life he wanted to live. He had simply chosen with more daring than most.

"You are a count and I. . . . " She paused. "I want to be like a beautiful lady. You like me," she said, insinuating herself toward him, "better than the Countess—no? I want a place where you can come to me, where I can be beautiful."

"A beautiful lady," he said, starting up and pacing about the room. A cheap little trick wanting to play like the real thing. To be a high-class bitch just like all the other high-class bitches. "She wants to be a queen. A beautiful lady. My, my. A smile from the Count and she wants to be a countess."

"Stop it," she cried angrily. "You think I don't mean it? You think your Rosita is all lace panties? So pretty-pretty for you to come and play with. You think I want to go home to dirt and filth?"

They all wanted it—to leave the bottom of the dung heap and look down from the top. An expensive game, as he so well knew. When they had come to town, he and the Countess, they'd had to make the yokels into believers. They'd had to make it look as though they had money to burn, so they could make a go of it: a dude ranch to bring the rich. Sleek horses and fancy cattle and expensive, gaudy, impractical clothes, and choice food to lure those who wanted to play at being cowboys and cowgirls, but in an atmosphere of luxury. Once he had a clientele he could also pick up a little pocket money at cards. For who could say no to a little game with the Count? But things still stood on a thin edge. They needed time to get a reputation, to have people say, "We went to the most exciting place. . . . Utterly charming people. The Countess she . . . the Count he. . . . " Ah, yes, he was a count and very rich. And he must make her like a countess: a little schemer who deserved no better than to have her neck wrung.

"And wouldn't the Countess like to know what you're doing while you're taking such good care of your guests?"

"What kind of stuff is that?"

She responded with a little smile, and sitting on the edge of the bed, continued to look up at him. "What will you give me?"

"My shirt," he said, sitting down beside her and reaching up beneath it to the strap of her brassiere. "The shirt off my back."

She sat stiffly, turning away when he tried to kiss her.

He'd have to bluff it out. "A little romp," he said, finally getting the hook undone. And as he put his hand on her breast, he tried to coax her toward him. But she wasn't having any of it. She pushed him away. And there was in the darkness of her look, the stubbornness of her lip, something he could neither get past nor push out of the way. He sat there, all desire gone, a chill at his vitals. The garden had become a swamp, treacherous. The meaning of her little endearments was suddenly quite naked to his eye. She had thrown herself at his feet, hung upon his every word, and shy, but willing, had worshipped his very footprints. He had fallen for it, though he knew one woman well enough to know them all. Caught. Trapped—between two tigers: one would bankrupt him and the other would kill him. Both would bleed him to death. He had violated the one law he could not afford to break: never to let life get mixed up with the work, always to look down at things with detachment.

"Give me my shirt," he said, getting up. If being a count meant anything, it meant that he didn't have to put up with that kind of crap. He'd get the police after her. If she said anything, he'd say it was a pack of lies. A few well-placed bills had an amazing way of bringing truth around to your side.

"Oh, you want to go," she said, jumping up, grabbing his pants before he could reach them. "You want your things." She rushed to the window, threw open the screen and sent the pants to the alley below. She took off his shirt and threw it down after them. She turned around, stood in the window giggling. "Now he has no clothes, *pobrecito.*" Then she laughed, pointing her finger at him. Laughing as he stood there in silence. Then she came toward him, smiling now. She came and stood before him, and pushing him until he stepped backward, made him sit down on the bed. Then as he watched she took off her brassiere and then her panties. She came over to him and knelt on the bed, kissing him, fondling him.

"Rosita," he said, lying down, taking her in his arms.

She laughed. "Does the Countess do what I can do?" She rolled over on the bed, as though in play. But before he got to her, she slipped out of his reach and stood up. "If you don't give me money," she said, "I'll make trouble."

He leaped up and caught her by the wrists. "Bitch!"

"I'll scream," she said.

He slapped her hard across the face. "Yell," he commanded, and struck her again. They'll come running, he thought, and hit her again.

She tore out of his grasp and sobbing, yelling, raced toward the bathroom, but he leaped onto the bed and down and cut her off. She ran toward the door of the room with him after her and, turning the key, nearly got the door open before he grabbed her and threw her aside. "Help," she yelled, as he seized her by the neck. "He's killing . . . me." But clawing him, kicking, biting him on the shoulder, she wrenched herself free and tore into the closet.

He was bleeding where she had raked her nails across his face. As he stood, panting, wiping away the blood, he could hear them coming. Then the door flew open and he saw the Countess, her face blanched, knife in hand.

He could almost feel the point in his naked flesh. Her eyes put holes in him too. Cold fury. No hiding. For Rosita, no more lace panties. A flash of rage went through him. She had him. But where did she come off to take a knife to him? "Come in," he said, making a low bow to the lady. "Now we're all here."

Rest Stop

Before I got my eyes open, I found it there under me—the car, moving and going. First waking up, I find it there under me. Moving—and soon as I look out the window, I see what it is now that's moving along outside. I took a look. Was a wrecking yard this time—cars going past, some right side up, some upside down. Whsst. A cemetery with the trees standing over. Then a field of corn stubble going brown, and a barn, boards all gone gray bare, leaning into the wind. We was coming to a town, but I couldn't tell whereabouts.

"Slow up," Ruby says to Webster. "There's a filling station up ahead."

He slowed and we all looked out for it, but it was shut up tighter'n a drum, like they'd all gone off and left it and wasn't nobody there and wouldn't never be. It was early, the sun coming on, but not up over the edge—too early for the grasshoppers to be stirring.

"What'll we do now?" Ruby says. "The kids're going to be waking up and squalling for a bite to eat."

"Look in the sack, Papaw. We still got some of that day-old, ain't we?" Webster says.

I wrestled round till I got the sack open and they was two bread ends, kind of dry, still in the paper.

"I thought there'd be more'n that," Webster says. "But that'll have to keep 'em till we get on home. We'll be home before nightfall."

"What'll we do then?" Ruby says. "Store'll be closed. We can maybe stop and buy something in the grocery." She opens up her purse and starts counting the money into her lap. "This here's all I got—one dollar and forty-two cents."

"Emma can feed us," Webster says. "She'll keep care of us this one night."

Home. All on a sudden there it is, right in front of my eyes. The old house with the porch sagging off to one side, and the chicken yard out towards the back. And I'm working towards the house, and all the time it keeps on moving back. But Webster says we'll be home before dark. Josh'll be waiting there, I'm thinking, but

Ruby says, "Goodness, Papaw, you know Josh's been dead and in his grave these two years."

I was just thinking it, and it was like Ruby come along and snatched it out of my head.

"Lord, he don't even know what he's saying," Ruby says to Webster—says it low, but I can hear. "He can't even remember Josh was dead 'fore we ever come away."

And I'm a-wondering, How the devil did that ever get out of my head? I didn't hear me saying it, so Ruby must've been waiting and snatched it. Josh'll be there, I'm thinking, even if Ruby knows I'm thinking it. I can see him. He's laying there in bed under the patchwork, kind of closed up in hisself now, being sick. Can't hardly breathe now and his voice comes rasping out. But sometimes his eyes fire up. "Git me a lump of coal," he says, clawing out with his hand. "Git me a lump of coal." Ever'body they stand stock still, he looks so wild, the spit on his lips like a dog gone mad. Emma tries to gentle him down, but he sets up and tries to talk some more, and he starts coughing and choking and spitting blood. The insides of his lungs is all black dust like he was turning into a lump of coal hisself. There was nothing for it but to fetch him what he wanted, so Jemmy he goes off for a lump of coal. A good big one is what he brung home. "If I can't do nothing else, I can fetch him a big one," he says to me after. He sets it on the table next to the bed and Josh looks at it and he says, "When I was born, they should've put chains round my legs and drove a spike through my chest and made me fast to the wall of that tunnel down there below. All my life down there in the mine, picking and a-digging. My life for coal. Coal to feed the fire. They should've chained me. Coal for the fire and fire for steel . . . and my life for coal. . . . "

Rachel starts stirring and whimpering in the seat, curled up next to me, and naturally that starts Billy to thrashing around too. "Here, come up to me," Ruby says, reaching around for her. She's all sleepy-eyed, just kind of whimpering. "Here now," I tell her and give her a boost; "up you go with your ma." She just sets there in Ruby's lap rubbing her eyes and fussing.

"You want something to eat?" Ruby says. "Papaw, give me one of them pieces of bread."

"Here, sugar," she says, when I get it for her. Rachel takes it in her hand and holds it like she don't even know it's there.

"Eat your bread, honey," Ruby says.

"Better eat that," Webster says. "All you're going to have till we get to home."

Rachel she just sets there whimpering and fussing, not even looking at the bread, and then it just falls out of her hand onto the floor.

"What'd you go and do that for?" Webster says, right sharp. "That's what we got to eat."

The car jerks off the edge of the road, 'cause he's looking at her instead of where he's going.

"You better watch what you're doing," Ruby says, "before you land us in a ditch."

"There, honey," she says, cradling her arms around Rachel. "Don't cry now."

"She don't quit that squalling, I'm going to give her something to cry about," Webster says.

Meantime Billy's setting there in the middle of the seat all staring sleepy-eyed, not saying a word. I open up the sack again and give him the other piece of bread. And he sets there, quiet, nibbling round the edges. . . .

The children will've growed some. Emma's youngest weren't but three or four—I'm trying to think. Little curly-headed thing, eyes the color of flax flower. And the oldest weren't more'n fifteen. "Now you get the insurance," Josh tells her. "They got insurance for when I go, and it's five thousand dollars. The policy's right in this here drawer. And when I'm gone, you take that and you tell 'em you got the insurance and they can give you the money. Leastways I'll be worth something when I'm dead." She goes to 'em and takes the paper. They shake their heads. "I got the policy," she says. "He told me to take it, 'cause you got the insurance on him." They just shake their heads. That company don't even exist no more—that's what they tell her. Just like the money has took fire and gone up in smoke. "He told me about the insurance policy," she says. "Gone out," they tell her. "What'll I do? she says. "You go ask the government," they tell her. "We got nothing for you." "All the men you got the insurance on. . . . " "Was a no-account company," they tell her. "Go ask the government. . . . "

Ruby picks up the bread and brushes off the dirt and shows it to Rachel. But Rachel don't want it and Ruby gives it to me to put back in the sack.

"Why ain't there been another filling station?" Ruby says. "I ain't seen nothing going past but fields and fenceposts."

"Look on the map," Webster says. "We should've hit a junction 'longabout here somewheres."

Ruby sets Rachel next to her on the seat so she can open up the thingamajigger and get out the map. She rummages around, pulls it out from underneath the little pistol Webster keeps there just for having it handy. One time we spied a cottontail right by the road and Webster he slowed down and grabbed that little pistol and shot it clean through the head, right from the car. Made a dandy stew.

"What was that town we was in?" Ruby says, trying to get the map open, and spreads it out on her knees.

"Look for Centerville. We was suppose to've turned at the junction fifteen miles out. That's what I been looking for."

Rachel starts in crying again.

"Look here," Webster says, "you start in with that and I'll bust you one."

"You leave her alone," Ruby says, chopping out at him. "You

want your bread, honey?"

She don't want it. She don't know what she wants. "Here, you come on back here with Papaw. You set right here on my knee." She comes and sets real still. . . .

"Emma," I says, "you take the land, plant you some beans, and hope for the rain. The well's gone out. Water's bad. Leachings from the mine has got to it. Chickens all died last spring, all excepting one and she follows me round the yard. I tell you, she puts up a awful racket when I go on in the house. And the drought made the beans to scorch. But you plant, you and Jemmy, and maybe you'll get you some beans." That's what I tell her, all the time thinking: If all your labor don't go for nothing. . . .

"What was that town near? I can't find it."

"I know we've come more'n fifteen miles," Webster says. "We must've got off the road somewheres."

"What're you going to do now?" Ruby says.

"Turn round and go back the way we come."

"You mean we got to turn round and go all the way back?" Ruby says. "We'll never get home before dark thataway."

"What d'you want me to do about it?" Webster says. "You got any better idea? We done missed the turnoff."

Sometimes you go one way, I'm thinking, and then you got to turn and go back all the way you come. Sometimes you go wrong traveling somewheres and sometimes you go wrong just staying put. It's a study. . . . "You see, you see where it's going to take you," Ruby says, crying. "Same thing'll happen to you—you'll be laying there sick and dying. Who's going to take care of Emma and the young'uns now Josh is gone? And if the black lung don't kill you first, you'll get trapped down there in the tunnel." "What d'you want me to do?" Webster says. "Only thing I know is digging coal." "Think of me," Ruby says. "What'll I do with these two babies it happens you get trapped down there in the mine? A rock falls and you get cut off or the gas explodes and leaves you trapped, dying of hunger and thirst and the air all filled with poison." "What d'you want me to do?" Webster says. "Let's us go somewheres else," Ruby says. "Let's us just pick up and go. . . . "

"Lord," Webster says, "I hope we got enough gas to get us home. This needle keeps on jiggling around loose. I can't tell a damn thing."

"You'd looked where you was going," Ruby says, "we wouldn't't've missed the turnoff."

"You just shut up," Webster says. "I got me enough troubles without none of your bad-mouthing."

I don't know about it, I'm thinking. This car's taken us a right smart of a piece, all the way back from California. But you can't put your dependence on 'em. Had a green Ford when we went up to Chicago, but it had a shimmy that like to wore out the tires. Then the fuel pump went out and the generator and pretty soon here it was the carburetor. Till Webster he says, "I'm going to get me another car before I try doing any more driving." Took awhile—Ruby saying, "When're you going to get that car?" "What d'you think you're squawking about?" Webster says. "You like to busted a gut trying to get here." Ruby starts crying.

Tell the truth, didn't none of us want to stay. We was all for picking up and taking off any blasted minute. Sun hit them Chicago bricks and like to stewed you in your own juice. Open all the windows and take off all your things and set around in your skivvies or maybe go set out on the front stoop, but the sweat hangs onto you and it wears you out to breathe. Nowhere to go excepting the streets. And somebody's forever coming along to pester—the police or the welfare or some preacher. About the only thing to do was wait till Webster got off at the plant. Then after supper him and me'd go on down to the Lantern and have a few and wait till a fight started up, then hang around to see how it was going to come out. Then go on home. . . . "What're you brats squalling about anyway?" Webster says, throwing the door open. "And where's your ma?" "I'm in here," Ruby says, raking back the bolt on the bathroom door. "That's where I am. And where in the hell've you been? I been waiting," she says, coming out, mad. Mad and crying. "Waited till I like to died. If he hadn't of been drunker'n a skunk, he'd have busted in the door. Comes in here and starts to pawing me." Can't hardly make out what she's saying, she's panting and yelling and crying around so much. "Who's been here?" Webster says, looking around. "Who d'you think?" Ruby says. "That pal of yours. He come around looking for you." Next day Webster brings her home a gun. "Anything happens, you use that." Then he says to me, "Come on, Papaw. Let's you and me go on down to the Lantern. . . ."

"When're we going to be home?" Billy says. First word to come out of him since he's woken up.

"When we get there," Webster says.

"Tonight," Ruby says.

"We gonna stay there all the time?" Billy says.

"You done asked that umpteen million times," Webster says. "Anyhow, we're staying put."

So if we don't run out of gas and don't nothing go wrong with the car, we'll come up in front of the old house. The steps is busted where the ice froze up in the cracks, and the porch has started in to sag like the house was sinking into the ground. And all morning the old place has been moving backwards the closer we get. The other time I was the one on the go, leaving it behind. Away in the green Ford to Chicago and then moving on in the blue Studebaker when we was heading out to California. . . . "What's that noise?" Ruby says, shooting bolt upright in the front seat and pulling on Webster. "There's a car pulled up back of us." Looking out the back window, there come three fellas, shining a flashlight. "Gimme that gun," Webster says. But soon as they seen us, they hotfooted it back to their car and jumped in and drove right off. "What was they after?" Ruby says. "They was going to strip the car," Webster says. "Come on, let's get out of here," he says, starting up. "We'll pull off on a side road somewheres." And we go moving on and the house keeps getting farther back. And when Webster couldn't get on at the plant and went to picking lettuce in the valley and we went traveling on up into Oregon, and the house was farther behind than ever. . . .

"I got to go pee-pee," Billy says.

"You just hold on a minute," Webster says. "We're coming to a filling station directly."

"But I got to go real bad."

"Ain't no place I can pull off. Look up there. It's going to come right around that bend in the road. You just keep watching."

"I just hope it's open," Ruby says.

I'll be glad to see that filling station, I'm thinking. Maybe they can tell us where we got off at and how to get back on the road. Sometimes they can tell you things at a filling station that outside folks don't even know about. Like the time we was out there in one of them western states. We was traveling through the mountains— bare red rock—all tired and the sap dried out of us, the kids fretting with the heat. And we stopped at a filling station and drunk a coke. "Any way to get somewhere cool from here?" Ruby says. "I feel like I'm going to burn up before we get done." And the man that was in charge, a right nice fella, he says, "You go on down to the fork and you take that dirt road and then you climb up into them hills. And when you get up to the top, you'll be in the grassland." It was a twisting, winding road all through the red rock—bare rock all cut out by the wind. But sure enough, up at the top the grass is deep and rich and the cattle are wandering round without even a fence to hold 'em in. And not far off the road there's a creek running through, brawling over the stones, meandering in and out where the trees are—sycamores, trunks the color of fawn skin, going white towards the top.

"Let's stop right here," Ruby says. "Don't let's go no further, but let's stop right here and rest."

We was all of us glad to get out of that car, after being cooped up for so long, and Billy he goes running barefooted through the grass, he's so glad to get out, and Rachel, even being so little, tries to follow.

"I'll fetch the blanket," Ruby says. "We can spread it out in the middle of them trees and eat our supper."

I set down and pulled off my socks and shoes. Felt good to wiggle my toes around a little.

"Let's go wading in the creek, Papaw," Billy says, catching hold of me by the hand. "Come on, Papaw."

"Oh, me," I says, getting my bones up off the ground. Billy he takes one hand and Rachel she takes the other, and we find a low spot and wade right in. It's cold water, cold as cold, but it feels good running over your feet, makes 'em tingle. And the water goes curling and wavering over all them bright-colored stones on the bottom. And a snatch of tune goes running through my head, from a long time back. Seems like it goes so far back I can't hardly tell where the music come from, welling up like a little spring under a rock.

> I want to go back where the sweet grass grows,
> And the breeze steps light through the valley.
> I want to climb out of this coal black hole,
> Take the road running straight so fairly.

I felt a little jab on my arm and there was a fly biting. I swiped it off.

> Lead me back, oh lead me back
> Where the deep water flows so purely.
> I want to climb out of this drag-down hole,
> Meet the sun coming up so early.

Then here comes another fly a-biting, and Rachel she starts crying, and Billy says, "Ow, that hurts." Seems like the flies is all over us, biting and stinging—mean flies—and we clamber up out of the creek, the flies still a-coming and a-biting. And right there in the grass is a dead cow, the flies festering around her.

"Run to the car," Webster says. "We got to get out of here before we're eaten alive."

"Oh, I'm so tired," Ruby says. "What're you going to do?"

"Keep on going," Webster says, starting up the car.

"Oh, there's never any place to stop," Ruby says. . . .

I see the filling station. It's open, sure enough, and Webster pulls on in. Webster he gets out of the car and goes round to the gas tank, and he and the filling station man look in the tank. And Webster asks him about the road.

"I'm going to have to get gas," Webster says, coming back, "and I ain't got but six dollars. Gimme that money you got."

Ruby takes out the change and gives him some pieces.

"All of it. We got to have ten gallons or we ain't gonna make it home."

Well, she don't want to give it all to him, but she does, and then she climbs out and takes Billy and Rachel round to the toilet while they're putting in the gas and wiping the windows. And pretty soon she comes on back and gets in the car, and the kids get in the back seat again. Then Webster comes, tearing open a pack of Camels, and he takes one out and lights it up.

"Where'd you get them cigarettes?" Ruby says.

"I got to have me a smoke," Webster says, "if I'm going to drive any more. My back's hurting and I got to have me a smoke."

"You spent the last money for cigarettes?" Ruby says. "What're we going to do when we get home? That's all the money I got. What'll we do to eat?"

"All right, all right. We got to get home, ain't we?"

"We won't never be able to stop. We won't never be able to stop. . . . "

"You quit that. You just quit that."

But she don't pay no attention to him.

And he just smacks her a hard one on the side of the head.

It's like she don't even notice, but she turns cold white like all the blood has drained out of her body. Then she puts up her hand, feeling of her cheeck.

What'll we do when we get to home? Seems like you can't tell what's going to happen in the next minute, let alone tomorrow or next week. I see the house. But where's Emma? Where's the kids? Josh, you're the only one there. And Ruby, what're you going to do? Reach over and open up the thingamajigger and take out that pistol and shoot it once and shoot it again. And Webster he cries out like he's hurt hisself. "I'm tired of traveling," Ruby says, her hand dropping down to her lap. "I'm just tired of traveling."

The Wayward Path

Soon as she saw what it was, she ducked down the side street and came home the back way. Somebody was moving in. She could spy out through the torn place in the lace curtain and see furniture coming out of the dark opening in the great orange ark that filled up the street. A sofa appeared, walking down the ramp, two legs at either end, rearing up to mount the steps. Two chests, gaping in the middle where the drawers went, lumbered down the walk. A sleek table sauntered by. Came a fat chair and a three-headed lamp. Furniture marching in to take possession of the house: Miss Bessie Stephaney's house.

—Think of it, Bessie—Sibyl Gunther said, —strangers. Coming to take over your house. You have to keep a sharp eye, Bessie— For sometimes you could look out and catch them—strangers coming in close, to where they hadn't been before. And if they didn't see you, you were one look ahead. Bessie wouldn't know a thing about it. Instead Miss Bessie was saying, "I'm going to bid six spades." She could see her plain as day, sitting across from her: round face with two pink spots of rouge on the cheeks and the shine on her forehead coming from her good humor over her cards. She always went set, too, trying to push her luck. Letty Turner was bringing round mocha tarts, and Bessie would insist on having some. "I'll take just the teeniest piece of that, they look so good." She couldn't turn down a sweet any more than a child could. "Now Bessie," Letty was saying, "you know that's not good for you." Then her jaw went stubborn, as usual: "This little piece won't hurt me a bit." And they had to let her have her way. . . .

She would have to spy out again to discover who it was that would be coming up the walk and going past the front stoop and into the rooms, making floors creak where nobody had set foot these many years. She couldn't recollect how many. Trouble was, time buckled up like an accordion and ten years got pleated into one. 'Twas hard to sort things out. Old Mrs. Bice had had it—Bessie's sister, and then the house went to her feeble-witted daughter, Sarah? or maybe Clara. Clarissa? But they put her away, packed up her life all in one basket and took her where they take people out of your ever hearing of them again. Then the house sat empty under the rain and snow, tangled up in lawyers. She'd seen how things went with it, letting an eye trail over it now and then, watched how the vines and creepers twined up along the porch, choking the posts, and how the weeds made a wilderness of the yard, saw how stones put out the windows one by one and how the weather beat it down, stripping off the paint.

Mercy, she hadn't even put away her things. She took off her cap and her brown jacket and put the gunny sack up on the table to have a look at the morning's collection. One good bottle, a skinny blue one with gold on the label. She could have had all the whiskey bottles she wanted, people throwing them left and right in the alleys and lots, but they didn't count—ugly brown things. —They couldn't find your poems, Bessie— She'd done everything just pat, so it must be she hadn't wanted anybody to find them. Sly, she could be sly. . . . A piece of red paper, some packing cord, a piece of metal, heavy—she couldn't say what it was, but it had a good solid roundness to it and not a bit of rust—two little boxes, good and sturdy, the right size for buttons and pins, half a dozen magazines with the covers torn off, a rhinestone earring—she held it up to let the light play on it—and a pencil with the eraser used down. And, ah, she'd nearly forgotten. Reached down into the pocket of her jacket for the Canadian penny; bent toward the light to look at the date. 1917. A good old one, too.

Through the torn place in the curtain she saw that outside things were still coming: beds and mattresses, boxes and more boxes. Then she saw who would be her neighbor. A woman stood in the yard holding two little girls by the hand. Children in the house. And there'd be a man, too, no doubt, coming directly. The house, bright with new paint, had been waiting for them. One morning, after she'd come back from her rounds, made early before the trash men came, she saw ladders leaning up against the house and men on the roof, ripping and hammering. There never was such a racket. Then they tore off the trim from the porch and took down the rotting pillars and built it all back up again. Painters came with brushes and buckets. An old man with a sickle took out after the weeds. . . . She'd have to keep a watch: somebody would be coming.

—It was knowing she was going to lose her toes that made her do it—Sibyl Gunther thought. It would have been too strange, parting company with something that was you, never knowing when you might have to let go of something else. Bessie had left a note telling how she wanted everything done, down to being buried in her transformation. She'd never even let on she was going bald. (Letty Turner went to a beauty shop twenty miles away to have her hair dyed, but all the girls knew she did it and let her go right on pretending.) They found her in the bathroom, with the gas heater turned on. She'd put a rug underneath her so she'd be comfortable.

She put the bottle up on the shelf with the others, so many there was hardly room. But she hadn't a blue bottle. There was a piece of amethystine glass, a jar she'd found in the cemetery, and a china vase fished up out of the sea near the Virgin Islands from when the slaves had rebelled and thrown in all the dishes. The sea had fingered it and twisted it out of shape. Perfume bottles, medicine bottles, too, of all sizes—they were the easiest to find. —The man will be coming directly—Sibyl Gunther said.—In the mornings I'll scoot out before he ever sets eyes on me— He'd be going out to work, all neat and proper in a suit and carrying a briefcase, maybe. —Dust— she said, and blew the dust off the china vase, which she prized. Dust on everything. She ran a finger down the side of a green wine bottle. —You may as well go out collecting dust— she said. —That's what it comes down to—

A man and a woman and children in the house. She'd never go near them, no indeed, never set foot in the door. She'd not gone to call on her neighbors for more years than she could remember. Couldn't even tell you their names any more, save for the Russoms across the street, who'd kept on in the neighborhood, waiting to see which would go to ruin first, them or it. One by one the houses had gone down. The big white one with the leaded glass windows where the mayor used to live. —John Corbett, I never saw such a man for joking. Not a serious bone in your body— She saw a huge lively man with a red face and a great meaty palm to shake you by the hand, to thump you on the back with. The porch was falling apart on the dark brick that used to be Jesse Ormsby's. —Matilda should see it now. Listen to her and you'd have thought 'twasn't a fit place for humans to live. But then nothing suited Matilda, she was so uppity up. Tried to run everybody—ran Jesse—would have run the bank, too, if they'd let her— The gray frame with the pillars, where the Snyders used to live. —Clarence a lawyer and having no better sense than to get tangled up with a trollop like that. Julia went where? To her folks in California, most likely, after she left him— They were all the big houses: carved up into apartments now.

Sometimes she looked into the open doorways as she went past and saw the children's toys lying in a clutter of bent and broken things and spied a woman who'd gone thick in the middle and flabby, dressed in shorts, hair up in curlers, working the vacuum over the rug and looking like something had gone bad right under her nose but she had to go on smelling it. And she walked past quick as she could before the stink of diapers or whatever disagreeable thing frying in the kitchen could choke her. Once in a while she'd say a word to one of the children scrabbling in the dirt out in front. The little ones looked at her with solemn faces, all eyes, like owls. One of them had burst into tears when she was trying to be friendly with him, so she didn't stop very often. —It's the looks of me— she said. Folks took her for a man more often than not, dressed as she was in her corduroy pants and jacket and cap, her hair cropped off short.

She wouldn't talk to anybody if she didn't want to. "You're a proud woman, Sibyl Gunther," she head John Corbett say to her, and remembered how her toes felt when she had danced with him once. —Well, John, you were right. I was proud at the beginning and I've been proud ever since— There she'd caught him. Ha!—just in time to see the man going up the walk, a tall fellow with dark hair and an easy stride. —I'll scoot out in the morning before you— she said —but you'll never measure the length of my pride— She'd come to town with her head high in those days, newly married, on the arm of the town's fire chief. And led the waltz at the firehouse and been invited to all the parties and gone out to the roadhouses to play at the roulette tables. For Edward was a man to gamble. —Liked to throw your money around, Edward— Generous and fun-loving, a man for a good time, a sporting man. Blessed too much with good looks, mind you. The cleft in the chin was what did it with the women. —You always liked the best of everything, Edward. Good whiskey and a good cigar—

It was the sheriff knocking at the door that night late in the winter. She couldn't make out what he wanted, he looked so hang-dog and wouldn't come straight to the point. Warrant for his arrest? Edward? He must be crazy. Bootlegging. She hadn't known a thing about it except that all sorts of people were doing it. Some said it was a frame-up to put off the revenue men. They said all the bigwigs in town were in on it. And they made Edward come to trial and sent him off to prison. She never saw him after that, the stranger she had married. Alone, with the child, money all but gone. . . . The only thing she had left of him was a rug made from the head and pelt of a polar bear he'd shot on a hunting trip up in Alaska. And she could see that fierce white shadow moving over the whiteness, unseen, hunting perhaps, white fangs ready—but hunted too.

—So there it was, John Corbett. You kept on talking to me, but what about the others?— Gave her a job, he did, in the city hall. And didn't that set the tongues a-wagging. She got to help take the census one year. Worked at the polls for the Democratic party during the elections. John saw to all that, till he ran for the state legislature and lost by six votes. Chewed over the bitterness of it till he died —So that was the one thing left I had to keep hold of,

John—my pride— It was hard on Neva growing up with the disgrace on the tongues of the town. And she couldn't live down having a father in the penitentiary. Wanted to go around with the high school boys that cruised around in their cars. Wanted to be popular. Wanted to run with the best in the pack, just like her father. —That was the trouble, Neva. Letting all the boys into your pants.— She went off to college, too, for boys with faster cars.

And who remembered all that now? People coming and going in the town, dying off and being born. The Reverend Warren Kemble was gone too and she wouldn't know the present minister if she saw him. Reverend Kemble had sat in her living room, had come by a time or two even after she'd quit the First Presbyterian. He had sat on the sofa with an aura of disapproval around his head like a cloud of gnats. She'd left a missing place in his church. He liked his church full, the pews all packed close and the hymns sung out in good round tones. Let people sit there looking at their neighbors and they'd keep each other out of mischief. Such was the power of religion. But she wasn't going to sit there under the eye of anybody. And what harm did he think it likely she might do—lay a curse on the cattle and afflict the babies with the milk sick? But the Reverend Kemble didn't come back after a time. And the town let her alone. . . .

. . . let her alone except when the mailman brought her the tax notices twice a year. When she saw the envelope in her mailbox, she was all in a quiver till she'd opened the envelope to see whether or not they'd raised her taxes. And even when she stood in the assessor's office to get her receipt, she trembled lest a voice speak out, "And how is it they missed you in the last assessment?"

The town came to her once a year at Christmastime with a basket of canned goods, a plucked turkey nesting on the top, and Mr. Toby Sheets on the doorstep, nose red with cold, stamping the snow off his boots, taking time off from the gas company to head up the Good Cheer Fund. "Hello there. Merry Christmas. Look what we got for you." "Ah," she got to say, "that's very nice of you to remember an old woman," talking to him as though she were talking on the telephone. But all the time he was standing there, she looked him in the eye to see what he was thinking and what he might be about to run off and tell to somebody else. She ate turkey for a week after.

—They're all done now— she said. She watched the men put their dolleys and mats inside the truck and get into the cab. Slowly and with a grinding roar, the great orange truck moved up the street. Inside the house they would be unpacking all the boxes, putting things away in the cupboards and closets. And there'd be more things. —Oh, you'll be surprised all the things that pile up over the years. They'll sit in the attic and the basement— Sometimes you didn't even know what you had . . . till one day you'd come across it and it'd be a new discovery. Sometimes you tried to sort things out and throw some away. Oh, but it was hard. She found things in the trash that people tried to throw away and brought them home—valuable things, too. She had drawers of calendar pictures and buttons and old Christmas cards and ribbons and coins and scraps of cloth and bits of lace—some things so old they were worth money. —It's seeing what you've collected is the main thing— she said. Sometimes people didn't know what they were keeping and what they were throwing away.

And so she had gone her way, and the town didn't say anything when she got up early and put on her mannish clothes and took her gunny sack and a stick to keep off the dogs and went along the alleys rummaging through the boxes and barrels. She was careful not to let anybody see her if she could help it.

For she had secrets. She had awakened one morning to the strangeness of things. First she discovered she could talk to her cat. Alone, they had things to say to one another. She had understood when the cat came to her asking where she ought to have her kittens. —Why, puss, I'll get you a box. You needn't worry— The cat felt better, she could tell right away. When the kittens were born and were lying in the box, little blind grubs with the mother cat purring warmly over them, it seemed to her that when she went back to the things she was used to, they were all strange. Even the birds, when she thought of flying, of lifting wings in flight. Or plants, with their invisible factories making food of sunbeams. Some days she would go out to the vacant lot next to hers to spy on the dark life in the grass, the little plants and insects that had their unknown connections, some breathing in life while others breathed it out.

And whenever she thought, bits of the strangeness came to her. And she grew strange to herself. —I won't talk to anybody I don't want to— she said. Lots of people you talked to it was like plugging into a switchboard and picking up the receiver, giving out your hellos, how-are-yous. Then when you were through, you pulled out the wire and put down the receiver. But when she reached down, she found invisible filaments or tendrils that could go from one eye, one core to another and would have remained past all separations. And deep in her imagination she found the thought of another man she might have loved, or perhaps a woman. She had her secrets, all right, and she had to keep on her toes for fear she might be found out.

—Why here I am, not doing a blessed thing— she said. Now the neighbors were inside she could go out to the vacant lot and see what had been blown or thrown into it—maybe a scrap of wood for the stove. She was stooping down in the weeds when she heard the children coming. Squatting down, peering out through the grasses, she saw the two little girls swinging their arms, heading right for the vacant lot. They ran into its wildness and went roaming through the weeds and bushes, bending over now and then, looking the way she looked for things. For, as she watched, that was in her memory now, the way she'd gone hunting for things as a child and found treasures—a bit of tree bark to be rubbed against the pavement till it was the right shape to sail in a puddle, a piece of colored glass that made the houses and the weather green or brown, shells and pebbles, an unknown part from an unknown machine. . . . They'd come upon her directly if she did not get up and flee into her house; but memory held her fast.

"Annie, come look. Look what I found," she heard one of the little girls say.

And thinking she'd see what it was too, she stood up. Both little girls gave a shriek.

"Oh, I didn't mean to scare you," she said, trembling. She should have thought.

"I found a bird's nest," the bigger girl said, breathlessly. "It fell out of that tree up there and it's still got a little piece of shell in it." She was breathing very fast and it looked as though her heart were pounding in her chest.

"Are you a witch?" the smaller girl said.

"Hush, Annie," the older one said, nudging her sister. "That isn't nice."

But Annie paid no attention and waited for her answer.

She laughed. "Just old, my dear." Even the laugh sounded strange in her ear. Not laughter—a cackle. Perhaps the child heard that. "When you live a long time, you get wrinkles in your face."

"Do you live there?" the older girl asked, pointing to her house.

"Yes, that's my house. And do you know what's in it?"

"What?"

"Many, many things. A conch shell you can hear the sea with. And money from the Sandwich Islands. And two little dogs that move when you put them close. And a picture of my old boxer that could do tricks—" It came out all wrong when she said it. She could tell by the look in their eyes.

Then the little one started running and the other took out after her. "She is too a witch, she is too a witch," she heard the little one yell.

That night the town came to her and stood in a ring about her. She could not see the faces, though in the flicker of the torches she could pick out here and there a forehead, a cheek, an eye, and then a ring of eyes. A figure detached itself from the crowd and started to parade back and forth, doing a little shimmy now and then. Neva, she cried, what are you doing here? Then the faces became those she recognized. Letty Turner and Matilda Ormsby. She caught sight of the sheriff, Phil Goodwin. And there was the Reverend Kemble. Ah, she said, and even you, John Corbett, for she could pick him out hiding in the crowd. She looked down and saw that even the children were there. And while she watched, one of the children picked up a stone and threw it. It came straight at her, and before she knew it, the stones came flying, thick as snowflakes. And the stones became a wall.

The Peach Tree

Mrs. Grenebaum started up from sleep in the nick of time to escape the pack of hounds that, having chased her into the daylight, still waited, panting, in the darkness at her back. She was frightened, puzzled to know what it meant. For not since the old woman's death had she had a decent night's sleep, and she wondered what it would be like to have another. She hadn't a bit of get-up-and-go; it had taken all her starch just to get through the night. When she pulled to get up, her bones had a reluctance to them, as though they'd been lying in a heap somewhere, disconnected, and she must put them together in order to rise at all. She sat on the edge of the bed with her eyes closed, thinking how pleasant it would be not to have to think at all, just this once, and feeling around for her slippers, letting her feet go at it blind. Then she heaved herself up, put on her bathrobe, and went to the window, hugging herself against the cold and groaning a little just below the voice. It was not done loudly—for Maudie was still asleep and she did not want to disturb her—but just enough so that, in case Maudie was on the verge of waking, she could hear and take the prompting to ask her how she'd slept, and Mrs. Grenebaum could tell her. But Maudie was dead to the world.

She cleared a circle from the fog of moisture on the window and peered out. Bleak, dark, snowing. Snow upon snow. The morning was thick with it, so that there was hardly any seeing into the yard. Even the peach tree was obscured, though her glance went to it right away, to the patch of snow beneath, where the old woman had been found, frozen to death. They might not have discovered her for days, but for her hand and arm sticking up out of the drift, as though to make one final snatch at life, the fingers folding in defeat. Mrs. Grenebaum shuddered. Nobody ought to have to get up in the morning and look out to see a hand pointing up out of the snow. She had thought at first glance it was merely a dead limb under the peach tree; and Oh God! that was what it was. She could not get over it. Of all the places in the wide world, the old woman had to choose her backyard as though it were the only place she could properly die in. Like enough she had done it out of pure meanness.

Once the idea suggested itself to her, Mrs. Grenebaum could almost believe in it. There had always been an odd edge, a corner of perversity about the old woman. Now and again she had come upon her poking about in the weedy patch she called her yard; the old woman had acknowledged the dry, brittle stalks as though she herself had sucked all the juice out of them.

"I used to have the prettiest flowers," she'd said once, "the deepest, vividest roses and iris like orchids, but people kept pickin' 'em and picken' 'em and wouldn't never leave 'em alone, so I figgered I'd show 'em. I'll just plant me some cactus, says I, and let 'em try pickin' those." And looking to where the old woman pointed, Mrs. Grenebaum could just make out in the middle of the tall weeds the spines of yucca and prickly pear.

And she'd stood there, the strangest little figure, so proud and feisty for all her get-up, the ill-assorted husks that covered her. The gray turban that for years now had hidden her hair, so that nobody could tell any longer whether she had any. The olive-drab wool coat held together by a great safety pin at the neck where the button was missing. (Maudie had sneaked over like a thief in the night to lay that coat on the old woman's doorstep so she wouldn't know where it came from; otherwise she'd never have taken it. "There was still a lot of good wear in it," Maudie had said, as though it had come with a certain quantity that must be got out before one was entitled to throw it away.) Black corduroy breeches, dull and smooth, from which the wear had been got out, coming down to just below the knees and joined by cotton stockings that made two skinny little black stalks down to her shoes. Shoes so discolored and misshapen they looked as though they were turning back into the earth they walked upon. Indeed, she herself might have emerged from underground, from inside an old tree stump going soft with the grubs.

"Well, all I know is," Mrs. Grenebaum had said, "I never in my life begrudged my fellow creatures a flower or two." The moment she said it she could have bitten her tongue.

For the old woman's face fell apart. Her eyes still kept a certain fierceness, owing to their blue and their depth in two bony caves; but her mouth took on the timid sadness of the mouths of goldfish. She screwed up her nose and snuffled once rather loudly as though she might burst into tears. She didn't; but Mrs. Grenebaum could see she was all in a quiver, what with plucking at the threads of her coat sleeves and wiggling her toes inside her shoes.

"Well, Beulah," she said, "you can spare a few, all you got." This time she sniffed. "And I got all this big yard to take care of myself—ever since I started farming here, as I call it. No man around—wouldn't have one. I do everything myself."

She didn't want people helping her. She clung to her independence until some extremity in her circumstances wrenched it from her grasp. She might struggle up the hill with a twenty-pound sack of potatoes she had bought in town and only if she were on the point of collapse accept a ride from a neighbor. Even then she would refuse to let him carry her potatoes to the door for her. And when, that fall, she had run out of money to buy coal to heat her furnace, she kept on as though in defiance of the universe. She gathered twigs and brush from her lot to burn in her fireplace and even climbed up in the trees to saw off the dead branches. Mrs. Grenebaum had seen her doing it a time or two. She was able to warm a room in her house—the rest she closed off. But she must have been cold a great deal of the time, for she at last submitted to having Mrs. Grenebaum save for her the newspapers she would otherwise have thrown away. And then, though she did not actually say anything, but because Mrs. Grenebaum could tell from the pinched look of the old woman's face, she began setting out for her the leftovers from her and Maudie's supper. "Bring the jar back," Mrs. Grenebaum told the old woman, who simply nodded. And that was the last thing either of them said about it.

"You don't imagine she's starving, do you?" Maudie said one morning as they watched the old woman take up a pile of newspapers Mrs. Grenebaum had put out for her on the top of the incinerator.

"Don't know and don't care," Mrs. Grenebaum said curtly. Her sister had an expression—pale, clouded gray eyes looking up at one, a knot of worry above her nose—that asked only that things be different from what they are. She saw the brows sweep up from the little gust of shock.

"Beulah, how can you? Oh, look," she said, still with an eye out for the old woman. "Her shoes are all full of snow. I don't see how she walks."

Mrs. Grenebaum gave a shrug, rejecting pity, annoyed with Maudie, with the old woman, somehow with herself most of all. There seemed always to be a question whose unsettled state left her open to a furious impatience. It was quite pointless to be cruel to Maudie, who was as simple as a sparrow. As for the old woman, all the years of living alone had made her a little crazy.

"I don't believe she's starving," Mrs. Grenebaum said, as though that was what made the difference. "Every day I take and put a piece of our supper in a jar and set it out there for her on the incinerator. And I make her bring the jar back, and I scald it. I wouldn't give her any of my good dishes, I wouldn't."

"Why Beulah, you're not afraid the old woman'll give us a germ, are you?" Maudie asked with mild surprise. "I don't believe she'll give us a germ."

Some fear of pollution, contamination—catching her death: possibly it was just that superstitious and irrational. Mrs. Grenebaum only fumed and did not know quite why.

"Do you know what happened?" she burst out. "Last week the pipes to her bathroom froze and burst and got water all over the floor. She can't even take a bath. And how's she going to get them fixed, I ask you?" She looked Maudie straight in the eye.

"I don't see that you need to get so worked up about it," Maudie said, finally averting her gaze. "I'm sure she'll manage some way."

"She can't take care of herself. She'll hang onto that wretched little house till it crumbles over her . . . "

"You can't blame her for wanting to stay where she's been for so long and keep her own things. . . . I'd almost be willing to give her that old chamber pot of Mother's," she added reflectively, "if I thought she needed it."

"When she hasn't got what will keep her alive. . . . It's pride," Mrs. Grenebaum said with furious impatience, "—pride that goeth before a fall."

When the old woman did not come back for a week, not even to get the oddments of supper put out for her, Mrs. Grenebaum was in a state. She roused herself from a sickbed, where she had taken an ailing back, put on her boots and coat and gloves, and braved the weather. Two days before, a blizzard had come and whirled the snow into drifts that came above the tops of her boots in places. "And what am I doing outside?" she wondered, "—bad as I feel. Fool!" she told herself. She crossed the old woman's lot like an intruder. Hers were the only footprints. The dogs had been there, of course, leaving their tracks behind, and a faintly acrid smell; but no one, not even the mailman, had come besides.

She had to take off her glove to knock at the door. Her knuckles made a hollow rap against the wood in the cold, aching so after a moment she had to put her glove back on. There was no answer. She looked about for a stone to pound against the door, but everything was buried under the snow. "Sibyl," she called, hammering the door with her fists, "are you there?" She waited, listening to silence; again no response. Perhaps the old woman hadn't heard or else mistook her thumpings for the work of the wind. Once again she pounded at the door and called at the top of her lungs. "Sibyl, are you there?" She might just as well have spent her labor trying to waken the dead. Horrified, she thought, Maybe she is dead. Maybe I ought to have the sheriff come and break in the door. But then, she considered, it had been years since the old woman had let a living soul come inside her house. There might be nothing wrong with her but the cold weather and her own natural stubbornness. Fancy trying to get the old woman to let her in; she ought to have had better sense and saved herself a tramp through the snow. Only once in her life had she been inside the old woman's house and that seemed to have been an age ago.

Now downstairs in the kitchen, Mrs. Grenebaum could tell from the creak of the floorboards above that Maudie was stirring. The cocoa was already made, and she brought out the white china plates and cups with the red cherries on them, the "cheery dishes," as Maudie called them, for she had bought them to have something bright to look at first thing in the morning.

Outside, it was nearly dark still and the snow was coming steadily—indifferent—shrouding earth and veiling sky. Mrs. Grenebaum felt a sudden chill. Maudie was coming down, and not feeling equipped to talk to her just then, she escaped down the back stairs to the cellar to get a fresh jar of jam. She opened the large cupboard extending from floor to ceiling and stood for a moment surveying the jars of fruit and jam she and Maudie had put up that fall. The trees had borne so heavily that even after they had heaped fruit upon the neighborhood, they had had to watch some of it decay on the ground. A suggestion of that wealth came from the jars of plums and peaches filling the cupboard, gleaming red-purple and gold in the dim light. But as she stood admiring them, the past intruded upon her.

"Hi there, hi there." The voice seemed to have come from the heart of the peach tree itself and Beulah Grenebaum, on her knees working in the garden, had been startled.

"Hi there, whatcha doing?"

She stood up, and walking over to the tree, peered up through the leaves and branches. There, framed in her window, stood the old woman with a towel swathed about her head. "Didn't know I was up here, did you?" she said, as though she had put one over. "I was just done taking a bath and stopped to look out and there you were. Whatcha doing?"

"Working in the garden," Beulah Grenebaum said, wondering if the old woman made a habit of spying on her. She held up her soiled hands.

"Oh, you've got a garden," the old woman said, as though she'd discovered America. "Why that takes real gumption—it do indeed."

She whistled several tuneless, irrelevant notes under her breath and said, "I used to put in a garden, but I never could get a blessed thing to grow. Just the weeds—they were always a-plenty; think of that. I put the seeds in the ground nice as you please and waited and waited for them to come up, but all I ever got was the blasted weeds."

"Maybe you got a bad lot," Beulah Grenebaum suggested.

"Must be. These here storekeepers'll cheat you blind. You got to watch 'em ever' blessed second and then all your labor's likely to go for nothing."

"Maybe you didn't water them enough."

"Oh, I watered 'em," the old woman declared. "I watered 'em with my sweat and I watered 'em with my tears. But if ever anything got above the ground, the weeds choked it."

"There's always weeds."

She had been young then, "Beulah" to her husband, "Mama," to her babies, and out of pity, out of guilt, she had gone to the old woman on missions of neighborliness. And once, carrying her a pan of ripe peaches, golden apples of the sun she had herself picked from the tree, she had gotten all the way inside the old woman's house: walking through the weeds to where it sat at the back of the lot, climbing the stone steps and entering the little stone porch, narrow and dim as the opening of a cave. She saw a blue feather or two in the empty cages hanging from the ceiling, relics from the time the old woman had kept birds, and noticed in the flowerpots lining the ledges bits of dessicated stalk in the hard solid clumps of soil. And she stepped past the threshold covered with the bear rug, the great head baring its fangs against all comers, formidable, though the fur had been worn away in spots.

She sat for a spell behind the drawn blinds in one of the old woman's overstuffed chairs, from which the flowers had faded and the springs threatened to pop through the upholstery, and listened to her tell about her childhood and her growing up, before she had made her disastrous marriage. They'd all lived in the big house then, where her mother had kept her from the age of four at music lessons and embroidery. "Those are piano hands," her mother used to say, and would never let her climb the trees in the backyard or play with her brothers out in the mud. And the old woman showed Mrs. Grenebaum the little carved spinet she used to play. It was hopelessly out of tune, the keys all yellowed and cracked, with several unwilling to play at all. And she brought out a coverlet made from pieces of the dresses her mother and sisters had worn, pieces of taffeta and silk and velvet, sewed together with lemon-colored silk thread and embroidered with golden strawberries and appliqued with green felt leaves. They were all gone now, all her nine brothers and sisters; she, the youngest, was the only one left.

"I'm not used to company," the old woman had said then, as she sat scratching her leg, making long red marks with her nails. "All my friends are dead—does that scare you?" And before she went on, she had given Beulah Grenebaum a long look, no doubt to see what was in her face.

"All I know is the neighbors. And I better warn you," she said, "the Perkinses on the other side are a bad lot. Mr. Perkins runs the taxi, the only one there is, and in the dead of night when he's taking home drunken men, he robs 'em."

Listening, she had been indignant, would be now, though it seemed she must long ago have worn out her indignation, the list of outrages had got so long.

"They don't complain neither, because he's in cahoots with the police." She was now scratching her side, under the armpit. "And do you know," she said in a conspiratorial whisper, "I believe they's trying to get my house away from me. Offered me money for it once, but now they're up to tricks."

The old woman looked at her suspiciously. "Maybe you want my house."

"No, never," Beulah Grenebaum said with conviction. And she'd left the peaches and taken her pan and gone back out into the sunlight, leaving the old woman behind the drawn shades.

Now taking a jar of peach preserves from the cupboard, Mrs. Grenebaum climbed the stairs to the kitchen, to find Maudie sitting disconsolately at the kitchen table, turning the spoon in her cocoa. She poured herself a cup and sat down.

"I'm sure I'll never be able to show my face in the neighborhood again," Maudie wailed, after the moment had spilled over with her misery. "People will say we should have seen to it she was fed and taken care of. Every time somebody looks at me I'll know that's what they must be thinking."

"Heavens, Maudie," Mrs. Grenebaum said, prepared to give comfort, "it was my fault if it was anybody's. I had business to get the sheriff to break in the door. But I don't like to go breaking in on people that way."

"You don't think they'll blame us?

"No," she assured her. "If they do," she added, "it'll be for the wrong reasons."

"It's stopped snowing," Maudie observed, "and the sun's come out."

"In that case, I'm going to put on my boots and coat and take out and burn the trash," she said, leaving Maudie to console herself and drink her cocoa.

It may be I've been wrong all along, Mrs. Grenebaum reflected— putting the blame where it oughtn't to go. For hadn't the town come and got the old woman's husband and hauled him off to prison and ruined her happiness and spoiled her prospects? And even now Mrs. Grenebaum carried around the doubt he'd ever been guilty. Whatever the case, the old woman had divorced him and taken back her maiden name and clung precariously to her existence for the past thirty-five years. And was it at the cost of the old woman's suffering that she had bought her safety? No, she protested; then she said to herself, Yes, as much as anyone else who lives. But then, who indeed could claim to getting off scot free? The world was endlessly selecting its victims, the greater and the less. She lit the match and watched the flames char the newspapers, lick round the beatings and stabbings and burnings and shootings, the everyday sack and pillage that made one want to grab his head and cry, "Chaos is come again." Ah, ah. All loss, all betrayal is death. And hadn't Henry been in his grave these seven years?

After she had done with the trash, Mrs. Grenebaum paused for a moment in the pure, brilliant cold, not wanting to go in just yet. The snow covered the ground and all the bushes and trees, but the sky was clear, and against the mountains the blue had changed and deepened into green. The cold was sharp to breathe as a hound's tooth, but each breath left the sting of ecstacy. A single crystal with an inward spark kept back from the cold: what was it that made life seem a luxury even in this bitter weather? Certain events she had celebrated with the snow: she had married in December and the following winter her daughter had been born.

The tree is bare now, she mused, looking at the peach, whose twigs and exposed branches made an intricate web against the sky, following the trunk till it entered the snow. And beyond? She tried to imagine how the roots lay in the frozen ground, and saw the woody crown descending and dividing into branches and diminishing into fine hair-like fibers. It was as though, beneath the ground, beyond the reach of sight, the roots formed an image of the tree itself, a nether tree, that in its descent into the depths and the darkness left her to surmise what hidden life?

In the True Light of Morning

The chirping of birds awakened him, getting in under the stillness and prying him up from sleep. It was still nearly dark and he did not want to wake up, but his body was on such poor terms with the bare ground, he found it impossible to latch onto sleep once he had let go of it.

There he was, the Reverend Ira Jack Dodgett. He sat up irritably and looked around, bird twitter in his ears. Noisy little buggers. He tried out his bones, rather stiff from the night on the ground, and ran his fingers through his hair to comb out the wisps of dry grass that had settled there. He remembered his coat, wadded up against the rock he had leaned on for a pillow, and shook it out. His Sunday good: a damp rag. Well, there was no help for it, he decided, no good muttering over it.

He stood up and brushed off his trousers, stretched and yawned, his eyes watering from the sleep still in him, took a deep breath for good measure and peered down into the face of Burl Canady to see how he was faring. He lay at his feet in the grass, his great paunch rising and falling to the rhythm of his snore. He could almost envy him that sleep, it looked, at least just then, so sound and undisturbed. Should he wake him up? Better not, Ira Jack decided. Better not to try to pull him up out of the whiskey he had soused himself in. He went off a little way to take a leak, then sat down on the rock to wait.

He liked this part of the day, the false dawn. It was a sweet time, still very quiet and dewy. Things held a certain promise—even the old farmhouse close by, faintly white, slowly emerging from the dark.

"Whoo—ee," he said aloud, softly. He'd really let himself in for a night of it. For a moment he leaned over the face of the sleeper, as though to read from it an explanation of why he'd spent such a bone-killer, hard on the old katootus. But the sleeping man had nothing to give away. A coarse face, reddened by sun and drink—there'd been dozens like it in the various bars he'd drifted in and out of, going from Texas north to the Dakotas, down to Georgia and back again. And he could fairly hear the laughing and the bragging and the swearing: "Goddamit, Bill Purdy, I just got me the neatest little bitch this side of the Alamo. Can smell out a chicken bone in a woodpile ten skunks a-been setting on. Can't hardly wait to turn her loose this fall." Work hard all day in the fields or on the road or in the factory, drink hard Saturday nights, and stagger home, swatting the chickens out of the way or the wife or the kids, whatever happened to be in the path. And strong. He'd known one who'd lifted up a tractor far enough to pull himself out, after it had turned over on him and pinned his legs underneath. Canady must have been strong, powerful, he thought, before it all went to his gut. Probably still was, in spite of the booze. Those fellows died hard. God knows, Canady had dragged him over half the creation before the night was over.

It hadn't exactly been his idea to spend the night there with him on the ground. It was one of those unlucky chances that he happened to be passing by just as Burl Canady came brawling out of the bar into the street ready to take somebody apart at the seams. Ordinarily—believing that it was only good sense to let a man alone to get into his own kind of trouble—he'd have ducked the other way. But there were people around. And when folks called you "Reverend" and "Brother" and pumped your hand on the way out the church door, they were entitled to their ticket to paradise—things had to look right. For his pains, he had been dragged around half the night and finally led, footsore and weary, to this field, where Burl Canady had ended the jaunt sobbing in his arms like a child.

That was pretty hard to take, even rougher than hiking around. . . .
But right now he wished he'd wake up, so they could get on out of
this damned wilderness. He was almost tempted to waken him, but
the thought of the past night held him back. Well, let him sleep, he
decided. He'd been drunk times enough himself, Lord knows. A
boozer and his whiskey are not easily parted: that was the wisdom of
the shot glass.

II

He let his thoughts wander back to the first time he'd taken a
drink—good Lord, a long time ago. The evils of strong drink had
been dinned into his ears with such thunder and repetition, his curiosity had been put on the boil. Anything that bad couldn't be left to
the evidence of tattle and hearsay alone—he'd have to try it out to
make sure they were telling him the honest-to-God's truth and it was
as bad as they said. Leastways, it would break up the dullness and
the farm chores.

He hankered to know, but it was a long time before he stiffened
up his nerve enough to try to find out. As it was, his opportunities
were limited. He did have a friend, Charlie Cumber, who lived in
town and sometimes came out to the farm to swim with him in the
horse pond.

Though it was a risky thing to do, he asked him, "You ever in
your life had a taste of whiskey?"

"Sure," Charlie said, with a careless shrug. "My dad don't care."
Then he caught on. "Want to try it?"

He teetered on the brink of decision. "Can you get some? I mean,
they wouldn't sell it to you, would they?"

"Don't worry," Charlie said, "I know a guy'll buy it for me."

On a Saturday, when Ira's pa usually went to town for the week's
supplies, Charlie came out. Ira Jack couldn't keep the question out
of his face. Charlie gave him a knowing look and patted his pocket,
and Ira Jack led him back behind the barn. Things seemed to hush
down, the insects in the grass, the horses at the pond, as the summer
afternoon joined the conspiracy.

"Here," Charlie said, uncapping the pint bottle and handing it to him, "you try it first."

He put the bottle under his nose and took a whiff. Bitter stuff. "Uff," he said, after it was inside his mouth. "That's awful. Why'd anybody want to drink that?"

"You have to give it a chance," Charlie said. "Besides, you didn't get hardly enough to tell about. Take a real swig. Like this."

He watched with admiration as Charlie tilted up the bottle and drank, his Adam's apple working. Charlie handed him the bottle and he did the same. The bitter stuff burned all the way down, so much that he thought he would choke, and sat burning in the pit of his stomach after it got there. But he'd done it. After that, they didn't mention the whiskey again, but passed the bottle back and forth. He concentrated on the burning sensation it made going down, the way fire seemed to shoot through his vitals, spread out, and warm him.

"You ever think about the things girls wear under their dresses?" Charlie asked him suddenly.

No, he never had. He'd seen his mother's bloomers hanging on the line inside the pillowcases, but he'd never found them very interesting.

"You ought to see them," Charlie said. "They got lace and pretty colors. There's this girl lives next door. Works nights at the Wide-Awake and she hangs all her things out on the line weekends—brassieres and panties and stuff. I look at 'em over the fence when I take out the trash." He took another swig from the bottle. "Do you ever dream you're doing it?"

"Doing what?" he asked.

Then Charlie said a word that should have brought the lightning down to strike him on the spot. He'd once asked about that word and his father had whacked him so hard across the side of his head, sparks flew out of his ear. And then Charlie told him some things that shook loose everything in his brain and exploded it all up into the air. He'd seen horses and cows mounting in the fields, seen calves born and cows butchered, in fact, had come to know at an early age about things begotten, born, and dying. But that human beings did no different than horses and cows. . . . His mother and father. . . . Somehow it had never occurred to him. The thought combined with the whiskey nearly made him puke.

"Lord, I had some dream the other night. Woke up and it was straight in the air," Charlie said. "Ever have that happen? Like a toadstool after the rain. Happens at the damnedest times. Sometimes when I'm just walking downtown, not thinking about anything at all."

And then Ira Jack began to understand some other things that had been troubling his mind lately. He'd never given much thought to what people were like without their clothes on. You didn't let the body be naked very often, but when it was, you quick covered it up and put your mind on something else. But somehow, without his say-so, his body seemed to be carrying on a life of its own and leading his mind astray. Even the preacher had got wind of it somehow. As Ira Jack listened in church, he expected every moment Brother Crawdon to point a finger at him and make him stand up as a public example: "Look ye, at yon miserable boy. Look ye: a house of unclean thoughts, of temptation and the flesh. Look ye and stand back aghast."

His conversation with Charlie had thrown him into the most interesting speculations of his whole life. But suddenly he recollected. "I'm never going to do any of that to a girl."

"No?" Charlie said, with a skeptical look. "Bet you're scared to."

He denied it. "It's all settled," he said firmly, about me being a preacher, soon as I get the right kind of education." The word had an important sound, connected as it was to the sense of duty that marched him to the round claw-foot table in the dining room every weeknight to do his homework. "I'm going to this Bible college where they mostly go to church all day and they don't even allow you to hold hands with a girl."

"I bet you don't," Charlie said provokingly.

He felt a sudden chilling fear that Charlie might be right.

"What d'you want to be a preacher for anyway?"

"Because. . . . " He had to think a moment. "Because it's the best thing a human can be."

Charlie laughed and said he thought it would be more fun just making out.

III

It was a good thing his pa hadn't caught them there behind the barn; if he had, Ira knew, he'd have whupped the bejesus out of him. As it was, his folks had always looked down their noses at Charlie Cumber. Thought he wasn't the sort of person Ira Jack ought to associate with. Even had their doubts he was a proper Christian and came from a good Christian home. Charlie seldom went to church because, he explained, his family were Congregationalists, and there was no church for them in Mount Pleasant—as if no other church could decently house their souls. Sometimes, when he stayed overnight at the farm, Charlie went to church with Ira Jack, who ducked his head as Charlie sang the hymns with an ungodly nasal twang, managing all the while to keep a perfectly straight face.

In many ways, his folks were right about Charlie Cumber. Why they hadn't forbidden Ira Jack his company he couldn't guess to this day. The first time he got drunk, really stinking drunk, was in Charlie's company and with Charlie's help. But looking back, he found it hard to put the finger on Charlie. If Charlie hadn't been around, he would no doubt have done the job on his own. Charlie. . . . Ira Jack could almost see his face. Whatever became of Charlie? he wondered. One thing he could be sure of at least—he hadn't become a preacher.

"Oh, uh uh oh." Ira Jack gave a start, having been jerked out of his reverie. Down on the ground, Burl Canady seemed to be tangling with a wildcat, yelping and thrashing his arms in his sleep. Ira Jack waited for him to wake up from the nightmare. But the spasm passed; his arm relaxed and he went on sleeping.

Ira Jack settled down again to reflect on the first time he had gotten roaring drunk. He had, in fact, managed to kill two birds with one stone—gotten drunk and lost his innocence, or at least part of his innocence, in the same operation. He wasn't exactly sure of how much of the total quantity he'd parted with, his brain was so fuddled at the time.

It was during the county fair in August, the summer he graduated from high school. His folks had left him in town—a great thing—where, along with the other farm kids showing stock, he would spend the nights next to the animals, sleeping on a pile of clean straw right in the cattle sheds. This was in case any mishap occurred in the middle of the night.

The last night before they took the cattle home, he sneaked off with Charlie to go to a bar Charlie knew about. He went with a heightened sense of his own deceit. He had an image of himself as he was supposed to be—sound asleep in the stable, breathing in the smells of straw and manure and cows, those harmless and innocent creatures that knew nothing of deceit. Instead, he and Charlie were tooling along the highway in the Chevy belonging to Charlie's dad, past the stubble fields of winter wheat. He caught a ripple of light on the dark water as they crossed the Canadian River.

When they got out of the car and went in, they stepped into a darkness glowing faintly with red and blue and green lights that cast shapes of color on the tables, but made the tables, chairs, and people sitting at them darker shadows in one large shadow. There was a jukebox playing Hank Snow somewhere in the background, the waves of music seeming to hover among the waves of colored lights. They sat down at the bar and Ira Jack tried to make out the names on the labels of the bottles that lined the shelves behind the bar.

"Sure are a lot of different kinds," he observed. He rather liked the variety—the colors of the liquids that gleamed in the bottles, the shapes of the bottles themselves, and the names of the brands. He tried several of the names on his tongue, their sounds holding a strange promise.

"Lots of ways to take your poison," Charlie said. "That's what my dad calls it. What do you want?"

He had no idea how to plunge into that fascinating variety. He tried to call to mind all the names of drinks he'd heard, but the only thing he could think of right then was a mint julep, and he wasn't sure that was the right thing to order. "I'll have what you're having."

Charlie ordered a beer and a shot of whiskey to drink together. "It's called a boilermaker," he said. "My older brother told me about them. Says they're powerful."

It sounded all right by him.

After Charlie had ordered the drinks and paid for them, he let Charlie kid him a bit about the bad influence he was having on him. It was still early and few people were in the bar. The air seemed thick and rather heavy, and time moved sluggishly.

They drank one boilermaker, then another, and started on a third. Suddenly Ira Jack was aware that the bar had become noisy around him. It had gotten crowded without his noticing. Next to him, Charlie was singing the words of "Sentimental Journey," which was now playing on the jukebox.

The tune caught him up and in between slugs of his drink, Ira Jack sang the words with him.

> Gonna set my heart at ease

"Hiya, honey. Want to buy me a drink?" A hand slid across his arm, and as he turned to look into the face of whoever had put it there, he wasn't sure whether it was her scent or her image that he became aware of first, or whether her perfume had brought an image to his mind even before he saw her. The perfume was heady, almost as intoxicating as what he drank—an emanation her body seemed to stand in the midst of, as though it were the source. Her arm led into it—beginning with her fingernails, long and tapering and shiny red on the hand that rested lightly and pleasantly on his arm, then the curve of her forearm, and then the rather full white soft upper arm. It was the suggestiveness of that soft flesh that excited him. Her face, a mask of powder and rouge, neither young nor old, he scarcely noticed. It did not matter. But her arm. . . . And the suggestion it held was outlined by the little shell of sleeve of her black satin bodice.

Sure he'd buy her a drink. Why not? Next to him, Charlie, rather far gone, was singing, "Never thought my heart could be so yearny."

The drinks, having plunged to his own depths, had left him warm and loosened up and highly elated. Suddenly everything was hilarious. He thought of the cows back at the stable and laughed. What could be more stupid than cows; what more absurd than living with cows? He couldn't stop laughing. The more he laughed, the funnier it seemed. "Have another drink," he said to Satin Sleeves, who had put her arm around his shoulder.

"Those are pretty little doodads you got there," he said, putting a finger on one of the rosettes that bloomed delicately along the edge of the neckline of her bodice. He traced the whorl of the rosette with his finger, then moved to the next and the next as they descended to the point of her neckline. "Right pretty."

"You think so, huh?" she said, nuzzling him. Her hair whispered across his cheek and sent a thrill all through his flesh.

Charlie, no longer singing, sat with his head on his hand, as though he were lost in a stupor.

"I got prettier things than that, honey," Satin Sleeves said to him. "You want me to show you a few?"

As though in answer, he leaned forward till his eyes were directly above the rosettes. He had to catch hold of the bar in order to keep from falling off the stool.

"Come along with me, honey." She took hold of his hand and he slipped down from the bar stool. The floor moved as he put his feet on it. He staggered.

The door closed behind them, leaving inside the voices and the cigarette smoke, and the fresh air touched his face with a cooling breath. Though he had no idea where she was taking him, he followed along docilely as she led him by the hand. He had the impression of going over uneven ground and through weeds where it was hard to walk.

"Where we going?" he mumbled as the earth shifted and heaved under his feet.

"Not far, honey," she told him. "Just far enough."

He stumbled and very nearly fell over something that caught his foot, a wire maybe. He was afraid to look down and see, afraid the ground might move out from under him. They had left the circle of light around the bar and had moved off into the dark. There were no other buildings around. In the distance a few lights winked. "Where . . . you live?" he asked. "Let's go . . . your place." He was trying to talk through a mouthful of cotton.

"Couldn't do that, honey. That'd be trouble. Here, sit down— right here. It's nice out in the open."

She put her arms around him and pulled him down for a long kiss. He pulled away from her, inflamed to find her body, to discover it with his hands, to let them touch her white flesh. He tore at her bodice, pulled it open and burned all over from the touch of her breast. "Hey, easy does it," she said, "I got to wear that." Maddened, he jerked up her skirt and tried to pull down her panties. But his fingers wouldn't work and she had to help him out. He was dizzied by the fire in his blood. He had come to that dark and secret place between the thighs—that thrilling furry place. He fumbled madly with the copper button on the fly of his Levi's. They were new and stiff and the button dodged and slipped between his fingers, refusing to go through the buttonhole. He swore brutally, hurting his fingers trying to get under the button and get it open. At last, when he was nearly beside himself, he got it open and readied himself to climb on top. But all of a sudden, it was too late.

"Lord, baby," she said, "if you can't do any better than that, you'd better cut it off."

The next thing he knew the sunlight hit him in the eyes. He woke up, sat up, his head spinning like a planet. When he stood up, the telephone poles began to weave, and he was sick. When he was through retching and stood, eyes watering, trying to catch his breath, he had a sudden intuition of loss.

IV

As it turned out, Charlie was both right and wrong: Ira Jack didn't go to Bible college and become a preacher. He hadn't reckoned on the reception he would get when he came home. His brain was so fuddled and his stomach in such chaos it didn't immediately occur to him that he was going to have to explain why he wasn't in the cattle barns that morning. But he was spared the trouble of having to lie out of it. Talk about an unhandy moment to show up: when he came down the road, he saw his father out in the side yard killing chickens. The fowl, whose head he had just chopped off, was flopping at his feet in the dust.

If he'd had any sense, he'd have ducked around and come up behind the barn and gone in the back door, but he thought too late. His pa looked up, their eyes met like the ends of two electric wires touched together—he would have to have a hatchet in his hand— and in the next moment he was after him, raging, cursing, chasing Ira Jack down the road. He didn't hang around long enough to find out what his pa would do with that hatchet if he caught him. He just kept on running.

And for thirty years he'd been carried along by that initial momentum. Working at one thing and another, continually on the go, he'd covered a great deal of territory, always passing through one place on the way to somewhere else. Just before he landed in this spot, he'd been traveling with a carnival, running the Haunted House—fun and thrills for fifty cents. Moving floors, sudden gusts of air blowing up the girls' skirts, ear-splitting shrieks and screams, chains rattling—the works. It was easier than some of the things he'd worked at, like cutting timber in the pine woods of east Texas or following the wheat crop north with a harvester team. It was more decent than other things he'd done, like working as a yard cop for the Santa Fe, running bums off the trains, or trying to shake money loose from people who hadn't paid their bills. These he'd done from hunger, and not for long. But by now he was tired of hopscotching around. He felt like staying put for a while, maybe lighting on a place for the winter and living off the fat of the land.

While he was walking down the road into the town near where the carnival outfit was pitched for the week, the breeze picked up a scrap of paper and dropped it at his feet. He bent over and picked it up, and his eye was caught by the title, "The Light of Salvation." He went along reading the piece of tract aloud, "Oh, lost and weary soul with no place to go—Jesus waits." As soon as he read it, a light dawned. Jesus didn't have to bother waiting any longer—there was just the place for him to go: some little town where they couldn't afford a full-time preacher. He could be a preacher. Why not? All that Bible reading he'd done as a kid ought to get him somewhere. All he needed was a diploma and a new suit. Then he'd look for a little place with a church that needed a preacher and get ready to grab salvation for the sake of his food and lodging.

The little town where he lit was ideal. There were ladies with gold-rimmed glasses and fat upper arms, who were eager to feed him fried chicken and creamed peas and mashed potatoes with gravy, and their menfolk who wanted somebody to deplore sin and creeping socialism, and young'uns who looked at him with trusting faces.

"You'll find just good, clean-living folks here," the real estate broker, a large freckled man, told him, "—folks that work hard and mind their own business and don't stir up trouble—just live and let live. Some of them Communist fellows been riling up the niggers pretty bad some places, but we don't have any trouble here. They ain't uppity here like you find 'em some places."

"Sounds like a good place to call home," Ira Jack said, hardly knowing what he meant.

"We been needing some good preaching, though. The state the world's in—wars and crime and the young folks going wild."

"Oh, I know, Brother," Ira Jack said. "It's all grist for the mill."

"You have a good way of putting things, Brother. I can see you're our kind of individual. You can hit pretty hard on the drinking and the dancing. The folks are worried about their young people."

"I aim to. I aim to talk about sin."

He aimed to. He stood up in the pulpit and looked at the expectant faces in front of him: the men uncomfortable in their collars and ties; their women, glad for the chance to dress up a little, leave behind the housework and visit with their neighbors; and the children, who seemed to read their surroundings by their own light. Then he'd start in. "I tell you, friends, you are looking at a man who was once nearly lost in the wilderness. I was only a young boy when I . . . came to grief." And he found himself looking into their faces again, looking at the men who sweated in the fields weekdays, planting wheat and cotton and feeding the cattle, and at the women who tired themselves out over the cookstove and with chasing after the kids, and at the kids, all absorbed in their own growing up. And his memory went back to his own folks and himself as a boy. And suddenly he was watching the horses drinking at the pond and it was spring and the little colts with their great tender eyes were running on spindly legs in the pasture. I'm tired, he thought. All I want is a place to call home.

V

Though things were still dim and indistinct, it was getting lighter. Tired of sitting, Ira Jack got up to stretch his legs and take a look at the farmhouse on the other side of the field. From his perspective, it appeared livable, decent enough. Even the blank windows he saw as he drew nearer, and the darkened interior, didn't break the impression. It could have been any house standing empty. But the other side told him what he knew already. A great black scar ran down from the roof along the wall, where the fire had seared it. The back wall was gone entirely, the black interior a gaping hole.

This was what Burl Canady had dragged him to in the middle of the night, after he had come brawling out of the bar ready to kill somebody.

"You'll land up in the pokey," Ira Jack had told him, trying to put him into a more sober frame of mind.

"Kill the cops," Burl yelled. "Kill the dirty sons-of-bitches. Who d'they think they are anyway?"

Ira Jack shifted ground. "Come on home now. Come on, I'll take you home."

"Home!" the man roared. "You'll take me home? We'll go home all right. *I'll* take *you* home." And clamping on him a grip of iron, he had led him out into the night, led him down the red clay roads till Ira Jack thought they must be lost among the ghosts of trees.

"There's home, Reverend," the man said in a stricken voice. A complete change had come over him once they stood in front of it. "Oh, Annie," he wailed.

Ira Jack hadn't been able to see anything then. Now as he stared at the scars of the fire, a shudder passed through him. Burl's child had died in that blaze.

"I killed her, Reverend. Oh, I killed her. Scared her, the poor little thing. I wasn't going to hit her . . . I wouldn't've. Ran right into the gas heater. And her nightgown . . . I can still hear . . . still hear. . . ."

A sudden movement in the shadows and the two men had leapt back startled, as they caught the gleam of yellow eyes.

"Why it's Ginger," Burl said, in an astonished whisper. In a second he was down on his knees calling, "Here Ginger, here kitty. I won't hurt you." The cat, the only living creature connected with the house that had stayed behind, meowed once and melted back into the shadows. "She won't come," he whimpered, looking up at Ira Jack. And his shoulders heaved with sobs as he knelt on all fours on the ground.

Ira Jack tried to lift him back up onto his feet. "Come," he said, gently but insistently. "Let's get on back where you can go to bed." He grabbed him around the middle and pulled. The weeping man was unresisting, utterly limp, but very heavy, and he slipped out of Ira Jack's grasp and sank down to the ground. Then after he had half pulled, half carried him partway across the field, Ira Jack conceded that they might as well stop for the night. As soon as he took away his support, Burl's knees buckled and he sank down again.

"She wouldn't even come to me," he wept. "I used to feed her out of my hand. This hand." He held up his hand in front of him for a moment and clenched it, digging his nails into the palm. Sobbing and hiccoughing, he finally subsided into sleep.

Now Ira Jack stood bemused, looking at the derelict farmhouse. It must be bad, bad for a man to have such a memory, to have to think about it for the rest of his life, grieve over it, be reminded of it every time he looked at somebody's kid. If he'd done it himself, Ira Jack figured, he'd want to spend every minute drunk or asleep too. Poor bastard.

VI

The reason I'm here, Ira Jack thought to himself as he worked his

way through the wet weeds and sat down on the rock, is I'm a
goddam fool. Burl Canady was going to wake up any moment and he
was going to have one sweet dandy of a hangover. But facing a man
with a hangover didn't bother him. It gave him a queer feeling to
have stood within the aura of the man's encircling grief, as though
he might not be able to get out again alive, or at least not without
taking some of it with him. Like catching a germ. But even that nig-
gling fear did not account for the nasty taste the night had left him
with. Suppose you wrote them off as a drunken man's tears. . . . It
might have been all right if he hadn't given himself out to be something he wasn't.

With a jerk and a start, the sleeping man sat up. He moaned and
bent forward, leaning his head on his knees. "Christ, what a head!
Oh." Moaning, he rocked back and forth, rubbing his forehead with
the tips of his fingers. Then sitting up straight, looking around as
though he were waking up in a strange land, he said, "Where the
hell is this?" He squinted at Ira Jack, rubbed his eyes as though to
make sure he weren't an apparition, and said, "What's going on?
What're you doing here, Preacher?"

"You oughta know," Ira Jack said, a little irritably. "You're the
one dragged me out here. Last night. . . . "

But Burl Canady, glancing wildly about, suddenly knew where he
was, and turning, seeing the farmhouse, was in a frenzy.

"What're we doing here?" he cried, leaping to his feet. "Why'd
you bring me here, goddamit? Goddamit."

"Wait, wait," Ira Jack said. "Just hold on a minute." He put his
hands up in front of him as though to fend off a blow. "You got it all
wrong, Brother. I mean, you brought *me* here. Remember?"

But Ira Jack could tell from the look in his eye that Burl Canady
didn't believe him.

"I know your kind," he said slowly, as though he were speaking a
curse, and at the same time moved toward him. "I know what you're
up to, all you psalm-singing sons-of-bitches. How you like to catch a
man and point a finger at him. How you want to make him get down
and crawl . . . so it'll make you feel good." And he jumped him.

"Wait," Ira Jack protested, falling backwards, "I ain't even the
real thing."

Canady had him down on the ground, his hands around his neck. "I'll kill anybody who. . . . " He thumped Ira Jack's head against the ground, as though he would crack it open like a gourd.

It seemed to Ira Jack, as he struggled to free himself from the hands that gripped his neck, that the whole thing was a terrible joke. He's trying to kill me and I ain't even the real thing. Then he thought, Why he *is* trying to kill me. God, he's crazy. A flash of rage went through him. All right, you bastard, I understand your problem. . . . But you got no call. . . . He tried to tear away the hands that choked him, but the man had a powerful grip. As he struggled, forced to look into that red, intense face, the glazed but maddened eye, a wave of despair came over him. It seemed that he and Canady as well were caught in the grip of a dark and hideous error. He might as well be choking in the clutch of his own terrible ignorance.

A howl came out of him, and in a desperate effort, he kneed his opponent in the groin as hard as he could. The hands let go of his throat, and in that second's space he seized the man by the hair and, rolling over, slammed his head against the rock. In the force of his fear, his anger, he slammed Canady's head against the rock again. And again. The eyes turned up into his a look startled and wild, as though only then had they first seen him. What was he doing? He stopped, recoiling.

Ira Jack scrambled to his feet, panting, sobbing for breath, for a moment too amazed to do anything but gape at the body at his feet, as though he were expecting some further threat. "My God, I've killed him," he said in a stifled voice, and knelt down to where the blood was welling up under the dark hair and trickling down the side of the rock. For a moment he remained almost in shock, afraid to find out if Burl were alive or dead. Then he felt for the pulse. Almost sick with relief, he felt the heartbeat. He pulled off his shirt, tore a strip, and bound it around Burl's head to staunch the bleeding. What should he do? Burl might die if he left him there, but he had to get help. He propped him up against the rock that had been anointed with his blood and stood up. Burl would have to stay there till he got help. There ought to be another farmhouse down the road.

He half trotted, half ran down the dirt road that had begun to take on its usual red color in the moments before sunup. He ran till it hurt to breathe, then slowed to a walk. He was all in a sweat and trembling, his knees were weak. Though not from intention or malice, he had almost killed a man, had been brought to the point where he'd not only have killed him, but wanted to kill him. And what if he had killed him? Would he find himself rushing out of a bar somewhere to latch on to some other ignorant bastard to continue the chain? The sensation of the whole experience sent him reeling in the dark. He felt the dark closing round his eyes, as though he were sinking into the earth, to the depths of a gulch where only thornbushes grew and cracks in the earth were made by the force of pain and darkness boiled from the craters of volcanoes. And it seemed as though he would be swallowed up in the darkness and swept away into chaos. He might have been witnessing his own death.

It was just before sunrise. Clouds caught the light of the approaching sun and the sky was red, a great solid brilliant red between the trees, the color of fire or the color of blood, as though the world were to be drowned or set ablaze. Then, light whelming and whelming, the sun came up, showing up the scars of things past and perished, but putting things back together with color and shape, re-creating the world. "Glory," he whispered. A terror seized him like a tiger and tore him to shreds. And it was as though his outward shell had cracked and fallen into dust and left exposed what lay beneath.

Flight

An empty belly is all it takes to bring a man to grief—his own and somebody else's. At the moment, he could call that wisdom—or, at least, part of wisdom. Another part of wisdom newly come to Orlie Benedict was that even when your belly was full, your grief, yours and somebody else's, did not necessarily depart. It clung to you like glue, as though it had a craving for company. The source of his particular trouble was a mere table length away. Just Nevermind—he hadn't been able to coax a name out of him—sat opposite, tearing apart a piece of bread, eating wolfishly. Orlie watched him wipe up the last streak of egg yolk on his plate and stuff the bread into his mouth. Gaunt face, several days' growth of beard along the jaw, circles beneath the eyes like bruises. He turned his eyes away—it was too much like staring into somebody's window—and put together thoughts of escape. Let us flee, said the fly. Let us fly, said the flea. Let us get the hell out of here, said Orlie Benedict to himself.

He glanced down to make sure. Yep, he had it, lying across his knees even, sticking out on both sides, handy to reach in case he wanted it—the rifle he'd never let go of, the rifle he'd met him with, when unluckily he'd come wandering up the road. Casually, Orlie moved his chair back and reached down for his guitar. They made interesting partners in misery, at any rate, he with his guitar, Gauntface with his smoke-pole. But he felt better with his guitar in his hands. He'd picked up a guitar along about the time he was eight or nine and hadn't ever really put it down. Without it, he felt naked. Moving his fingers over the strings was a way of thinking, putting things into a shape and working them out before they slipped away. Right now he had a few to go.

Gaunt Partner in Misery, now that he had cleaned up the food on his plate, sat in relative calm, knuckles bent around the mug of coffee, as though he were warming his hands. "Can't recollect the last time I put food in my mouth," he said almost sociably.

"It can be hard on a man," Orlie said, having listened more than once to his guts growl. He tried out a couple of chords and sang:

> I'll eat when I'm hungry, I'll drink when I'm dry
> If the wandering don't kill me, I'll live till I die.

If Gaunt Partner had anything to do with it, it might be sooner rather than later. Hard on a man for sure.

"Funny thing," Gaunt Partner said. "I don't hardly know where I'm at." He looked around the room, then shook his head, as though he had come into a strange world—thinking he had awakened but finding himself in a nightmare. And no wonder. The place was a shambles: dishes, cans, and bottles swept from the shelves and lying broken on the floor; curtains ripped from the windows; papers, shoes, magazines thrown helter-skelter. And Orlie'd walked right up and into the middle of it, had opened up the door to a whirlwind. He strummed up a little tempest on the guitar. Then he backed up for a bit of melody, lighthearted, just as he had been, walking up the road, almost drifting through the quiet of the summer afternoon toward the peace of that farm in the late sun.

First thing he'd noticed as he came round the bend was an old pump under a shade tree, with a flop-eared hound curled up next to it. He looked over the barn—red once, paint flaked down to the bare boards. He liked barns—they had character, more than houses sometimes, almost as much as people. Some so clean and red and sharp they made you whistle—so fine and big the house that stood next to one was put to shame; others all gray and tumbledown, as though weather and neglect had got the best of them and it was only a question of time until they caved in. This was a barn on the way down, a little seedy, but the house was still trying, the paint recent enough to give it some credit. Nothing fancy, but perhaps you could ask a meal from it, in return for a little work, and a place to put up for the night.

He caught sight of a man out back behind the chicken house and went on past the house to say "Hi there," and wangle a meal. Then he stopped, was stopped rather—brought up sharp, the breath snatched out of him. His eye had gone on ahead and his thought had lagged behind. A lot of chicken feathers, he noticed. Then he saw what he had been seeing: chickens strewn around the yard, lying with that particular limpness that gave him to know their necks had been wrung. Who'd do that? he wondered, sickened by the slaughter. What kind of nut?

Transfixed by the sight, he hadn't gotten from the question to the thought of what he'd do next when Gaunt Partner came up with his rifle. "You ain't gonna get her," he told him, jerking the gun up. "Man, I don't want her," Orlie said, backing off, ready to get out of there in one hell of a hurry. "Just you wait. You get on in there," he said, waving the gun in the direction of the back door. "Look, fella, I didn't mean any harm . . . I was just passing through." "You're not about to go and bring the rest of 'em down on me." He's kidding, Orlie thought in disbelief. Been seeing too many bad Westerns. But it was clear he meant it. They went into the house. There was no arguing with a crazy man.

He hadn't been surprised to find the chaos of the house inside. Well, it figures, he thought simply, when he walked in, though he had no idea what had brought it all on.

"Sit down," he was told. He sat. It seemed as though he must have sat for a long time, long enough for the room to make him feel a little crazy himself. It made him jerk his shoulder every once in a while, twist in the chair. He found himself mentally returning cans to shelves, straightening the bent curtain rod and putting the curtains back up, sweeping up the broken glass. It was nerve-wracking to do nothing: for a time he was driven to making patterns out of the fragments of broken glass on the floor in front of him, staring at them until they came together in some way. Then almost gratefully, he found his attention absorbed by his hunger, that familiar reminder of his physical life.

"Mind if we have a bite to eat?" he ventured.

"There's food," Gaunt Partner told him, without apparent interest, bent over in a chair, gun across his knees, absorbed in whatever whirled in his head. Orlie's presence seemed to make little difference to him.

And though it had brought him into trouble in the first place, he was again grateful for his hunger. It gave him something to do. So he'd pawed around in the wreckage, found bread, not fresh, but edible, found eggs in the refrigerator, discovered the coffee can. The coffee, black and bitter though it would be, boiled on top of the stove, reassured him, the fragrance reminding him that somewhere calm and the simple routine of the evening meal existed. He had brought the two plates of food to the table and they'd broken bread together.

It might be, Orlie considered, that the food had had an influence for the better. He didn't mind his face so much now—it was looking halfway human. Some of the wildness had gone out of it, leaving behind a look of great weariness, as of spent force. Rather a young face, Orlie saw with surprise, the face of someone he could know. But the impression left when Gaunt Partner stood up. "Where did I . . . what's happened here?" Then he flashed around. "Where's Molly?"

"Steady, man," Orlie said, reminded of his danger. He had no idea who Molly was, but it seemed he had her to thank for some of his trouble. In his imagination he had run out the door and down the road. What to do. He tried to hatch an idea. Maybe he could do it the way they were always doing it in the movies. "You got anything to drink?" he wanted to know.

But Gaunt Partner wasn't paying him any mind, going on about Molly and where was she—the frenzy returning, if it had ever abated. Frantically, Orlie was rummaging through shelves and cupboards. Just my luck if he's so square he never takes a drop, he thought. Good sober lad—just tears things to pieces. He hadn't seen any broken whiskey bottles—a bad sign, or maybe a good one. If he had one, where would he keep it? As Gaunt Partner ranted on, he could have wept and raged himself. One more minute, he thought, and there'll be two of us. Under the sink, next to the potatoes, he found a bottle. Great day. He jerked off the top and took a swallow. Here's to you, friend, he said silently. The life you save may be mine.

Seizing an unbroken tumbler, he poured it over half full of whiskey, ran in a little water from the tap, and carried it over to the table. Should he or shouldn't he have a drop to hold himself together? Wisdom was tugging at his sleeve: what did he want to go and muddle his head for? But Lord, he wanted a drink! It seemed to him that he had soaked up in a single day all the wisdom he could possibly hold, so he allowed himself a dollop.

"Come on," he said, encouraging Gaunt Partner back to the chair. "A little of this will take you to the moon without wings." Gaunt Partner sat down with a moan, collapsed rather, like a sack of potatoes.

He must have been raving around quite a while, Orlie decided. How many hours, days? Strange to think of anybody doing it for very much time. He looked like he couldn't have a whole lot of raving left. But it might be that once he got caught up in the storm, his craziness had given him a queer sort of strength. Surely he'd have to sleep sometime. The whiskey might help him along. Get him drunk enough and he'd pass out. At least it couldn't make him any wilder than he was already. Or so he hoped.

Picking up his guitar again, he sang

> Rack falls the Daddy-o
> There's whiskey in the jar.

Gaunt Partner sat neglecting the glass, leaning his head in his hands. "Gone," he moaned.

Looked like he and the wife had come to a parting of the ways. Maybe she'd just packed up and taken off—that's what'd happened to his brother. Came home and found a chair to sit on and a bunch of clothes hangers in the closet and the cat meowing to be fed. He tried to get the feeling of departure, thought of the chair sitting there in the empty room. But he had no real experience. Even with his folks. He'd been born when they were old, and he couldn't grab hold of a distinct impression separating the time he'd had them from the time he hadn't. But he had learned some words:

> The longest train I ever did see
> Was a hundred coaches long
> And the only woman I ever did love
> Was on that train and gone.

There was a long silence, after which Gaunt Partner raised his head and sat up. Orlie took a swallow of the liquor by way of encouragement. But Gaunt Partner might as well have had blinders on, for all the good it did.

"I can't believe it," he said slowly. "I think it and I can't believe it." There was a long pause. "She had yellow hair," he said.

He'd sung about all kinds of hair and eyes. Black was the color of somebody's true love's hair. And somebody had dreamed of a girl with light brown hair. And somebody else had thought it over and found brown eyes so beautiful he'd never love blue eyes again. When you fell in love, even if it was only for half a week, you were ready to go on about the girl's hair and her eyes and her cheeks and her lips. Yellow hair was all right too. He could say that much. And he knew a little of things breaking up with a certain amount of regret. Not that his experience had been great.

> Once I had a yellow-haired gal
> Once I had a yellow-haired gal
> Things've gone wrong with my yellow-haired gal
> What has become of my yellow-haired gal?
> Yellow o my yellow o my yellow-haired gal
> She's long gone, my yellow-haired gal.
> Yellow o my yellow o my yellow-haired gal
> Yellow yellow yellow, yellow yellow yellow,

he sang, carried away by the pure sound of it.

> Yellow yellow yellow
> Sad and sorry fellow

> She's done come and
> > sad o sad o sad o
> > > She's done come and
> > mad o mad o mad o
> ooooooooooo
> > She's done come and gone.

There, he thought, delivered of song, that'll do for a jilting or a divorce. She smashes all the crockery and he—then he thought about the chickens. But who does that?

"Goddam it! What do you know about it?" Gaunt Partner said, bringing his fist down on the table so that the plates jumped and the tumbler of whiskey spilled all over.

"I'm sorry," he said, taken down. Gaunt Partner had turned away from him. He'd missed the boat, that was clear, but he didn't know how. He waited.

"She's dead," Gaunt Partner said. His back held considerable dignity.

"How did it happen?" he asked, thinking, I don't even have the right. . . .

But Gaunt Partner, becoming more lucid, seemed to be hit by the impact of things standing in the harsh light of greater clarity. "Good Lord," he said, standing up. "What's happened? I don't know where I been." He walked up and down the room, in front of the oil burner and past the doorway from which could be seen the brown painted chest of drawers and the bright squares of the quilt on the brass bed, then around by the sink where a faucet dripped, perhaps examining the damage done or maybe just seeing how the familiar had shifted and shown him strangeness. "Who . . . did . . . all this?" he said, holding out his hands.

Orlie let it ride. He'd know soon enough, know maybe more than he could use.

"And who the hell are you?" Gaunt Partner demanded, as though it had just now occurred to him that he didn't know.

"Orlie Benedict," he said, with a shrug—as though that answered anything. What else should he say? The fellow you told to get on in here. Tune picker. Wanderer. He shrugged again. Your partner in misery—one way or another he had been stuck with that.

But Gaunt Partner seemed to have lost interest in the question. "I don't know where I been . . . " he muttered, as though he were struggling to find his way back to a beginning. "Funny thing, you know," he said. "You think you know where you are . . . and then you don't. Like I fell off a cliff."

He probably didn't remember about the chickens, Orlie thought. Didn't even know he was doing it, most likely. And what was he going to think of it when he found out? But that would wait. It was just part of the aftermath, of the full ugliness of misery working itself out. Gaunt Partner had come back to himself and there was not a thing for him. Wife dead. Ruins at his feet. What was he, Orlie Benedict, supposed to do about it? Where were his friends, anyway, and his folks? Probably ran them all off. Once they started running, it wasn't likely they'd care to come back. Not that he could blame them. To run had certainly been his own first impulse—which only proved that most people had more brains in their feet than anywhere else.

"I don't know where I been," Gaunt Partner said. "And I don't know where I've come."

It seemed like a natural time for a man to pour himself a drink and dive to the bottom of the glass. Orlie reached for the tumbler, poured out another round.

"And I don't give a shit," Gaunt Partner said, as a sort of conclusion. Then he took up his rifle and sat there sighting along the barrel. Was he going to take a gun to his troubles? Orlie wondered. Shoot them away? Suppose one could. . . . He took his guitar again, from where he'd laid it across his knees, and sang:

> Oh, I'm gonna chase that wild, wild wind
> I'm gonna catch that rover
> Oh, I'm gonna chase that wild, wild wind
> Till he gives back my lover.

Gaunt Partner set the gun down for a minute and looked at him as though waiting to hear something he could tell him.

Oh, you'll never catch that wild, wild wind
You'll never catch that rover
What he takes away, he never gives back
The wind that blows you over.

He spat with disgust and raised his gun. "Shoot it," he said.

"Won't do any good," Orlie said.

"Shoot the whole goddam world."

"There's a power . . . " Orlie began. But his words were lost in a blast that went ripping through the front window.

"Careful, man, you want to kill somebody?"

Gaunt Partner looked at him with haunted eyes.

Orlie's heart thumped in his chest like a wild thing butting against the bars of a cage. And his fear spoke to him with a thought: It's him. He's the one who's killed her and now he's going to kill me. What else had he been ranting about when Orlie came up? From the midst of his fear, he spoke: "It won't bring her back," he said.

Gaunt Partner stared at him for a long moment. Then he set the gun down, leaned his head in his hands, and wept.

Orlie sat for a moment, letting his heart calm down. Death had brushed by his ear so close he had felt the whirr of its wings. Then suddenly he thought, I can go now. As soon as he knew that, knew it with a sense of release, the urgency seemed to diminish. He wasn't ready to go yet.

There's a power, he thought again. You sing a tune, by a mountain, maybe, and when your tune is done, the mountain is still there—it hasn't changed any and doesn't show a trace. Nothing is changed except maybe yourself for singing, and if anybody else happens to hear you, maybe something happens to them, but it was nothing you could know for sure. But what did that have to do with anything?

He let his fingers wander over the strings of the guitar as he tried to find out. It was a struggle—finding out. He had to wrestle to get the right note and the right word. To get them, he had to work till the spirit of the thing he was yearning toward and the music met. And sometimes he didn't know what thing it was he groped for in the dark. If he got to it, it was like making a cup out of his hands and catching something for a moment—and for that moment he became the music—but pretty soon the spirit splashed through, flowing on past. That was the power—the thing one could never wear out. Then he thought, If you could get it all in one tune, or even a dozen, it wouldn't be worth having. There seemed to be a comfort in that almost, that nobody could ever get it all, that the force was real, not some poor thin stuff he could wear out if he set his mind to it.

It's the same power, he thought suddenly. Gaunt Partner had had to look at one side of it, and he'd been looking at the other. He thought he saw now how they were joined.

Orlie glanced over at him. He was sitting quietly now, gazing out through the broken window. In the still light sky a crescent moon was visible. "You all right?" Orlie said. But the other did not turn nor answer.

I can go now, he was reminded. But still he wasn't ready. Gaunt Partner had gone out of his mind and now he had come back. He wanted a word—what was it?—he had known once and that still flickered somewhere in the back of his head. He worried around till he found it. It was a case of fugue—a flight from what was too much to bear. Fugue. Odd that the word should also be a flight of music. Then he thought, I'll take a little flight of my own. It took him awhile to get it. Then he sang:

> Loss of love,
> Loss of memory—
> Flight from the void
> Flight into the whirlwind.
>
> Flight from the void
> Flight into the whirlwind.
> Memory of loss
> Memory of love.

When he had finished, he saw that Gaunt Partner had his head tilted back, asleep. Not a matter for whiskey after all. Now it was time to go, to take flight himself. But still he didn't move. He sat looking into the face relaxed in sleep and found again something familiar—human. Maybe he'd get a better sleep if he were stretched out on the bed. Putting his arm around his chest, he half carried him to the bed. Though he muttered, perhaps in protest, he did not wake. Orlie untied his shoes and slipped them off, then unloosened his belt. He stood there for a moment watching him sleep. He had done, for the time being, all that he could.

On the Edge of the Desert

Purple cactus against a purple mountain—she was quite certain of that. But how could she describe the strangeness not only of the plants but of the dark quality they held in those surroundings? A luminous dark that came from within the plants themselves: purple darkness, but lightening into brilliance, joining with the brilliance of the mountains. Had she really seen it like that? Never again had she seen anything in that way. So that now she wondered if it had been pure imagination. A vision, perhaps, created out of her own sense of strangeness. But that didn't altogether explain the phenomenon. There had been something there that, whatever it had called up from the depths, had come to consciousness with the impact of experience. She could not have said then what had been evoked. There was, as she thought about it now, only the sense of powerful presence, the sense that she was in a place she knew nothing about. Unknown, therefore separate from her.

Always before, the landscape had been familiar ground, in which she grew also, like the plants. Against the planes of grass and sky stood Mrs. McWilliams' Boarding House, porch running along three sides. Behind it, the garden and the vacant lot, where three abandoned Fords sat, rusting in clumps of violets. The kids used to play in them, shifting gears and making motor noises, gathering speed. Back against the fence was a cherry tree she climbed each year to steal the fruit. About her own pillared house roses bloomed and lilacs, snowballs and mock orange; wisteria hung over the side porch, so that on summer evenings the dusky air seemed but the deepening of scent, that during the day was mixed up with the buzz of wasps and bees.

The sunset brought the purple martins arching over the evening to birdhouses in Mr. Shoebrook's yard. For alongside his garage he had made an elaborate two-story birdhouse that sat atop a tall pole. She wanted then to be a bird herself and to descend on one of the little perches and disappear inside to live with the birds. The most she could do was climb the mimosa trees. And once she had gotten stuck on the fence trying to get to the martins. Mr. Shoebrook had rescued her. And for consolation he had made for her a wooden boat to sail in the mud puddles when it rained. His workshop was a splendid place, though she had never been inside, for in it he made birdhouses, and her wooden boat, which he painted a pale blue.

Mr. Shoebrook had a little wizened old wife, who cooked on a wood stove and kept a parlor all closed up except when company came. She had been inside it once. A cold room, it smelled unused, as though no human step had ever gone inside until they opened the door. And the objects in it were, to her, like the things in church, where she had gone once with Miss Bessie Conoway. On the floor sat a great conch shell, smooth, shining flesh-pearl inside. "Pick it up, Rachel," she heard Mrs. Shoebrook say. "You can hear the sea inside." She picked it up and held it to her ear and there was the sea.

The blue summer ocean. Smell of salt and tar and suntan lotion as they walked along, feet sinking into the warm sand, as they tried to find, amid sitting and sprawling forms and the gaudy array of beach umbrellas, a spot of their own. Mama's skin was easily burned, so Mama sat under the umbrella most of the time and ventured out to take a dip once or twice during the afternoon. Meanwhile she, Rachel, roamed the beach looking for shells or waiting for the skirt edge of the foam to come up almost to her feet, to jump back at the last minute. And when the wave receded, turning over the bright pebbles, she watched the bubbles break the surface of the sand where she might dig for sand crabs—"wigglers" she called them. And then afterwards, the walk along the boardwalk, stopping to buy taffy or caramel-covered popcorn or to put a penny in one of the machines in the arcade that scooped up candy and sometimes gave you a shiny black-and-white china dog from Japan, but never a pocketknife or a cigarette case.

The rounds of summer. A whole cycle. The riches of the world flowing in at the same time she was sending deep roots into the familiar. Except once. Once on the Choptank River while the adults sat on the porch of Zeb Petrie's summer house, she had gone to the edge of the woods and seen a great shining green insect, like a huge grasshopper, and its green wings had shone in the dark woods. She had started to follow it, but she was afraid. She had gone back to the cottage to tell the others about it and convince them to come with her, for she could not bear to give it up, that marvelous shining creature. But they denied what she had seen. There was no such insect. Her father, Zeb, Miss Gwen all denied its existence. And what protest would hold up under the weight of that much adult opinion? She must have imagined it. And so she had been left to wonder what she had seen—what elusive thing. But the touch of the inexplicable had not marred the surface of things. Not yet.

But at the age of ten, coming from East to West, she had felt a sudden break in her experience like a crack in an egg. She found herself standing on the edge of the desert. All about her were forms of life she had never seen before: mesquite and desert poppy, thistle, yucca and joshua tree. And the cactus. Spiny, jointed forms of living tissue holding the precious water. They belonged to the land as she did not. And though she didn't know it at the time, something had to give way to make place for them. And for the mountains.

That was the pristine experience. It had come back to her with a certain clarity, the years having swept it free from surrounding detail. It was as though you walked on a road without noticing the surface; then when you turned back you found that wind and rain had uncovered various rocks and stones that had been lying just underneath, some gleaming like gems. It was quite startling, in fact, to see how things were never over and done with, how they kept a life of their own, taking on certain hues and textures and locations as they worked their way back to the surface. Startling, yes.

You had to acknowledge a certain power that lay within event—

the power to become experience. So the experience had come back to her, with the force of contrast. For now she was driving back to New Mexico for the first time since she had left. She was driving now—driving quite alone. It was the emblem of maturity, wasn't it? Getting your license—the mark of the rites of passage. A sign of control. Observe all signs, for the road through the mountains could curve dangerously and take you unawares. But she had come to be able to handle certain things of the world fairly skillfully—things like money and schedules and doing work and getting from one place to another: the array of necessities and conveniences that made it possible to survive from one day to the next.

When she saw the yellow sign with the red sun symbol, "Welcome to New Mexico, Bienvenidos," she felt a sudden joy. She was back again. The sky was magnificent, a drama in it, the great cumulus clouds like battleships. Its color was a turquoise she had never seen anywhere else. The quality of the light she was grateful to seize hold of again, a quality that illuminated something in her vision as well as the landscape.

Las Cruces had grown bigger than ever, the main street crowded with people and cars. Buildings, more buildings. It was the first place she had known in New Mexico. Her family had stayed there a few months with her mother's sister, who had, in fact, helped to bring them to the West—the land of opportunity. She hadn't seen her aunt and uncle for years now. The two families had quarreled and gone their separate ways and, in this world at least, would never see one another again.

She made her way through the traffic out of the city and up into the mountains. Ranch land. And she still kept the sense of joyful recognition—seeing as being—a kind of absorption in the landscape. Once it had come to her with the impact of experience. At the time she hadn't recognized it for what it was—the crack across the surface of the familiar, and her emergence, wet and scrawny—entirely newborn.

She could see her father driving the car that brought them there, a 1935 Plymouth. It was the end of the War and the car was as old as she was. He was driving and smoking a cigar, filling the car with the dreadful smell of it, so that she was quite nauseated. But she dared not say anything, for the stink of the cigar was easier to endure than his temper. The lights were on, though it was broad day, for there were too many amps in the lamps, as he explained to her. But the lights were to be the sign by which her aunt and uncle would recognize them as they drove from Las Cruces to meet them. It was just before they met that she had seen the cacti. She had wanted desperately to stop and look at them, but of course that was out of the question.

Her father had been dead for twenty years now. She scarcely thought of him. Perhaps she would not think about her mother either but for the fact that she was still alive. Her own life had gone in other directions. And she had quite happily buried all of what lay behind in New Mexico. So that the sudden elation she felt startled her. Perhaps it was the reconnection with the now-familiar. But there seemed a danger in it too, finding one's way back, finding that all that lay there had not settled down quietly and sunk to forgetfulness.

She remembered hearing once that Benny Gonzales had his own gas station now. And she was quite sure that the Texaco she had pulled into must be it. And quite sure that it was Benny himself who came up to see what she wanted. His face was older and he had gained weight. Though still good-looking, he bore little resemblance to the tall slender kid she knew in high school.

"I'll bet you don't remember me," she said as she paid for the gas.

He paused, looked at her with concentration. Then his face broke into a smile. "I think when I first see you, you look familiar. What are you doing here?"

"Just visiting," she said vaguely.

"The town has grown," he said. "Lot of bad times in the mines. Then suddenly everything opens up. I'm busy all the time now."

"That's good," she said, glad to see he was prospering. She asked about his wife and kids—she couldn't remember at all the girl he married—wished him well and drove the last few miles into town.

The town had changed, she had expected that. But she was not prepared—ideas were never preparation—for what she saw. She'd left the town full of ideas. Now, coming back, she found her stock greatly reduced. Even those she still held on to were continually tested by what was before her eyes; whatever she thought, it seemed that the world had to enter in, demanding something of her, like an insistent peddler.

Things change, of course, but the impact she had no way of gauging. The road winding, turning back on itself in a series of hairpin curves, evoked other journeys, some at night, one through a dust storm. But what had she expected to find at the top of the last curve, before the descent into the town proper? The same lone drive-in at the top of the hill, where the jukebox played "If You've Got the Money, Honey, I've Got the Time," and "Have I Been Gone Too Long?" Even had it been there, the main sensations would be missing—of being seventeen and feeling isolated in a small New Mexico town, but more than that, of being unable to express the feeling.

A large two-story motel that looked quite new took up a great section of what had been the empty space between the drive-in and the town. Crowding around it were gas stations, used car lots, drive-ins—cans and paper cups scattered along the route—all in a continuing flow of modernity that connected the town with the rest of the world. No longer a backwater, it was a stopping place on the way to California, connected by a new road. Once it had been cut off, the only people coming there being those for whom the town was a destination.

Beyond the general impression of the whole, there was little of the main street she recognized. The flagpole in the center of the intersection, the bank, though greatly enlarged, the hotel, the courthouse remained to position the street, give it its moorings and identity. But the facades of the stores had all been redone, most of the businesses having changed their mode of give-and-take with the world. Even her father's store, though still a furniture business, presented to the street a different name and character. As such, it was but a shell. She may as well have been seeing it for the first time.

She even found the stuccoed duplex where they had lived, where she had grown up, though as she drove up the street she thought it was gone. Hidden by a great billboard advertising a savings and loan company, the house emerged suddenly as she continued up the hill.

The change of perspective startled her, for the billboard most emphatically occupied what had been a vacant corner, a space of weeds and rocks, not wholly obscured by the whiskey bottles and papers that used to collect there.

And now she knew what was missing from the locale or what had been added that had changed its quality. Before, the town had had a certain pathos in its ugliness. Here in the mountains, where silver ore had been found, and then copper and zinc, a town had risen up. A boom town for a time. Not the fabled Seven Cities of Cibola with roofs of gold, the tales of which had brought the explorers. Rather a town coaxed out of the earth itself, of adobe brick. Tough, without pretense, tolerated by nature, but just barely—dwarfed by the mountains, reduced to mud or dust, depending upon whether it was wet or dry—that was the town. But now, there was an insistence that progress had been made, that there were those in charge. Nature was asked to wait on the outskirts and to behave herself.

Nearly all the streets were paved now. When she was a girl, most of the streets were dirt, and during a rain, the water ran down the back streets in little streams, eddying around the rocks. Thistle and desert poppy grew along the edges of some of the streets. And behind the stores, where the main street once had been, but which had been swept away by a torrent from a cloudburst in the mountains, the ditch it had made still remained. The thirty-foot ditch that ran a torrent when it rained. But a wall hid it; a new bridge had been built over it.

So that on her approaching her old house the shift of perspective had its full impact. She felt a kind of dizziness, as though the land had suddenly given way and, opening before her feet, revealed a chasm below. For, in fact, where was she now? Where had she come? The frozen-food locker plant across the street was gone. A rush of images came and went before her eyes. The woman there who had lost her left hand in the meat grinder. The scream, and afterward the gloved artificial hand. The woman was smiling at her as though the pain, the loss had never been. The house was there, it was true, but everything, the living experience that had flowed through it once, was gone entirely. Shells.

Once again, though in a different way, here was the crack across the surface of the familiar. For in her mind the town partook of the changeless. When you left a place, it seemed to her, it became your last picture of it, below which were stacks of other pictures. She had left, and the town had become like one of those ancient buried cities that lie unknown below the earth until it is discovered and the life that went on there painstakingly reconstructed. The life—she wasn't even sure any more what it was or how she could get back to it.

At least she knew where to begin to look. After all, her mother had stayed on in the town, her life absorbing the changes, maintaining the connection between past and present. Without a great deal of interest she had read from her mother's letters what had happened to one and another of those she had been content to let drift into forgetfulness:

> Gertie, poor thing, is in a rest home. Ninety years old and still hanging on. Frank—that so-and-so—got power of attorney over her estate, and he's living it up, let me tell you. And rotten to the core. When I think of the grief he gave poor Gertie. . . . Always a worry. It was all she could do to keep him out of prison. That he should be the one. . . .

Saturated with her mother's sense of injustice and envy came the changes of the world, along with her complaints that things were dull, there was nothing to do, no life to live. Discontent in the present a continuation of her discontent in the past:

> I never hear from Hilda. We were supposed to be such good friends. I think a psychotic change has come over her. That's all you can call it. But after Jack died and she had to give up the business—that was right after the operation. She had to have an eye removed, which isn't too pleasant to talk about and a glass eye put in. As I say, after Jack died, things there were never the same.

But what of such details? She didn't even know quite what she was looking for—something to catch hold of, perhaps. Her father and

Max, his partner who had cheated him, both dead. Henrietta, Max's wife, in the madhouse. And even Honey, the sister she had grown up with, who had shared some of her life, she hadn't seen for years. Married and divorced and married and divorced—Rachel could scarcely keep track of the men Honey had gone through. They were all scattered like so many dead leaves. And what were they supposed to mean to her now?

The town stood in the present—on which of the various levels would she find her Troy?

No doubt she had been putting it off, preparing herself, one might say. She had to ask directions to the small, newly built private hospital. In truth, she hadn't wanted to come back at all, she acknowledged, as she wound through the streets toward the edge of town. She hadn't wanted to be reminded again of the past. There was no remonstrating with it. Had it not been for her mother's stroke, she would have been spared all this—experience. What nonsense, she thought. One way or another, she would have had to look at her as the living connection—the living ghost, one might say, of the past.

The hospital was quite posh in its way, with an oval drive and a bed of roses in front. Just imagine someone taking the trouble to get them to grow, she thought, when cactus would have done the job so much more simply. And besides, she thought, there is something phony about those roses. Inside she found the usual paneling and false brick and vinyl chairs and tables with magazines, the decor of waiting rooms. She gave her name and sat down to wait for the doctor, who would speak with her.

She had very nearly dozed off before Dr. Herman appeared. "So good to have you here," he said, giving her a firm, rather meaty hand to shake. He had an agreeable, satisfied expression, as though he had just come from a good lunch and was still absorbed in its flavors.

She had a hard time getting him to speak plainly.

"Is she very bad?" she insisted.

He stroked a small mustache and grimaced as though he were working hard to bring up an opinion from a great depth. When he did respond, it was with a kind of evasive condescension: she was a child or a lost soul that understood but little of what went on in the world.

"I want to know her real condition," she demanded.

"Paralysis of the left side," he said, surprising her with a plain answer.

"Will she recover?"

He shrugged and considered. "I wouldn't like to be too definite at this point. At times there's an amazing strength, unlooked-for resources. Your mother is relatively young."

"She has a chance then?"

"I wouldn't rule it out. A lot depends on her own will to live."

"I'd like to see her," she said. She wanted to get away from him, for he was going to do her no good at all. Whatever the situation held, it would have to be met on its own terms—that much was clear.

"Along this corridor," he said, moving more briskly than she would have expected. "I have to go this way."

Her mother appeared to be asleep when they entered, but one eyelid fluttered open and half shut again. The doctor examined her chart. "I would suggest about ten minutes at the most," he said.

"Will she understand me?" she asked in a whisper just as he was leaving. But he failed to hear.

"I'm here, Mother," she said softly, so as not to startle her. She bent over her. The eyelid fluttered open again, and she heard a low sound from her throat, but whether a groan or merely a catch in her breath Rachel couldn't tell.

But she can't speak, she thought wildly. Of course she can't. She hadn't thought, no, hadn't thought of that at all. She wanted to embrace her. "Mother," she said. "Oh, Mother." But it was quite as if her mother had slipped through her fingers and was entirely beyond her reach.

When she left the hospital, she did not return directly to the car, but instead walked out along the road toward Gila as it wound around above the town. She walked out as far as Chloride Flats, at one time and perhaps still the place where lovers came to park. She turned to look at the town below, then left the road to walk on the land. A lizard appeared and shot under a rock for cover. At one time their quick scurrying had startled her: they moved like lightning. But it was one thing more she had become used to.

It was quiet up there, as of the first beginning. Cactus and thistle and ocatilla and mesquite. With a certain strangeness still in them. The first time, she had come as the child of the children of immigrants who had left their Jewish culture and religion behind them. But though they lived in this place, their eyes were turned toward what they had left behind, so that it seemed to her now they must never have seen this land. Not as she had had to look at it. She had grown up with the mountains, with this landscape, with its daily insistence that she confront it, though she had scarcely known what to do with it.

It had formed her mind, a mind made in the mountains, floating between those forces of ancient accommodation of life to its surroundings and the partial emancipation from them that could be called consciousness. But whatever she had done or become, it hadn't been enough. She wanted to discover the town; if she found it, she would discover something more of a mind. I know, at least, that whatever I find, it will be my own creation, she thought.

And she felt quite alone. Her mother lay suspended between life and death, and she stood suspended between past and present. It would be terrible if the dead had too much claim upon her. She did not want to be buried.

She was reminded again of the cactus. It was all around her; she had to walk carefully to avoid the spines. The prickly pear had bloomed and the fruit was already formed. The thistle was in bloom. It was quite a fierce plant, bristling with spines. The leaves were spikes and the calyx was covered with little fine needles, from which emerged the flower, as though out of that violence was born that intense and purple bloom. The plant, sharp along the stem, had seemingly fought its way into existence, stabbing out its leaves and conceding nothing in its flower. Brilliant. And ocatilla with red points, and on the cacti, pink and yellow flowers. Even in the desert, she thought, there was continuity of form, of life holding onto its precarious existence by preserving the precious water. For the moment, that was a comfort.